but George McAlister had been sick. Chances are he was hung-over. Rogelio Lopez wasn't the only person in town to go a little crazy on a Friday night after getting paid. Chief Taylor preferred to have a minimum number of men on patrol to prevent any lapse where trouble might spring up so we could be prepared. Seems he always called on me to fill in seeing how I didn't mind. It was something to do to pass the empty hours.

George often acted like a young version of me, except without the war experience. Too bored to work on a farm all his life and wanting to do something a little more exciting. He had built up his body so he didn't look like a pipsqueak, but he had no concept of death, certainly not the way I witnessed it in the trenches. It was dark and muddy, devoid of dignity, and stank of decay. He probably never thought about getting killed trying to stop a robber. Worse than that would be getting into the middle of a fight between a couple where the husband was madder than a hornet. He didn't think this wasn't a charmed life, and he'd have to work every day just to take another breath.

Praise for H. B. Berlow

"In the '30s, all towns and most cities had very little documentation required for police activity. Hell, around here as recently as the '70s you could arrest a felon by filling out a 3x5 index card with a simple narrative on the back. And it was perfectly legal to shoot and kill a felon if they didn't stop when you told them to. (That didn't change in the South until 1984.) So you are spot on with having your character concentrate on the street instead of worrying about lawsuits and heat from the brass."

~*James Montgomery, Officer,*
Garland County, Arkansas Sheriff's Department,
retired

Ark City
Confidential

by

H. B. Berlow

To Debbie:
Inspiration comes in many
forms. In this case, it
was your daughter. Thank
you for providing me
the opportunity.

Ark City Confidential

Cover Art by *RJ Morris*

The Wild Rose Press, Inc.
PO Box 708
Adams Basin, NY 14410-0708
Visit us at www.thewildrosepress.com

Publishing History
First Mainstream Historical Edition, 2017
Print ISBN 978-1-5092-1183-8
Digital ISBN 978-1-5092-1184-5

Published in the United States of America

Dedication

I am indebted to Larry Hammer
for the stories of the underground tunnels
and "Little Chicago,"
and to the Cherokee Strip Land Rush Museum
in Arkansas City, Kansas,
for the many research materials.

Chapter One

I had just signed out from my shift and was looking for nothing more than an Epsom salt bath. That's the worst part about being a beat cop, the toll it takes on your feet. We weren't as big-timey as Wichita or even Tulsa. There wasn't a patrol car for every guy on the force. City Hall had repeatedly said through countless administrations they couldn't afford it and didn't think it was all that important. Economics was the reason my feet hurt so bad.

I was no more than twenty feet from the Municipal Building when the kid ran up to me. I had seen him wandering around in the past, never knew if he had parents or where they might be. Social work wasn't part of my job description, plus I figured the kid was doing a decent enough job of taking care of himself seeing as how he'd not been brought in for any minor offenses. He had dark hair, dark skin, and big brown eyes. The cuffs of his pants were frayed, and I wasn't all that sure his shoes even had any soles. I figured he was Mex but he could have just as well been Indian, like one of the kids from Chilocco.

"Mr. Witherspoon." He kept calling my name like he was trying to remember it. Everybody knew my name on account of the fact I looked different. I was "that guy." He stopped just short of me, leaned over with his hands on his knees trying to catch his breath, practically wheezing, and then looked up. "He's doing it again."

Rogelio Lopez had a menial job at one of the mills. It seemed just about every Friday night, right after he got paid, he'd get stinking drunk and fire off a few rounds on the railroad tracks near the east edge of town. Got to a point where no other officer wanted to deal with him seeing how he was becoming an annoyance. Half of what we dealt with was nuisance calls. That was about the extent of the crime we encountered. After several weeks of this, I guess I was the only one who gave a damn. The kid smiled at me, knowing I was heading off to Rogelio's rescue yet again.

Straight on out Chestnut Street was where I usually found him. He didn't let me down. A bottle of something with an amber liquid in one hand, and a revolver in the other. The government was only just getting started repealing Prohibition, which meant Rogelio was in violation of two laws. I approached slowly, as I usually did. Just a silly old drunk Mex is all he was but it was my job to make sure he didn't harm anyone, let alone himself.

"Hey, Rogelio."

He whipped around fast, the gun at his side like a bandit from the old outlaw days. We were maybe fifty or sixty feet apart. The move was pretty sudden causing my heart to skip a quick beat. He was leaning forward, somewhat uneasy on his feet, almost to the point of falling over. The squint in his eyes made me aware he hadn't yet focused on whom I was. With all my facial scarring, it wasn't going to be too difficult to figure it out. Soon, there was a big broad smile on his face.

"Ah, Señor Witherspoon." I smiled knowing he

finally recognized me. He extended the bottle in my direction. "Want a drink?"

"No thank you." My smile matched his. We were just two smiling fools, only one of us was too drunk to realize it.

He spun back around, tossing the bottle in the air at the same time, a fluid move with unexpected grace. When it was at its highest point, Lopez flicked his wrist, turning the barrel of the gun up in the air, and shattered the bottle with a single shot. In his condition, it had to have been luck. If it wasn't, I could be in trouble.

"Waddya know about that?" He was half turned toward me, his wrist too flimsy to hold the gun still. He started to shrug his shoulders, almost giving up in defeat, when his arm twitched and the gun went off, the bullet splintering the ground about five feet in front of me. If I had a moment to think about it more, I would have realized this was the same drunk man I'd been tending to many Friday nights in the past. I would have reminded myself he had never hurt anyone and probably never would. But when a gun is fired in front of your feet, you don't have any spare moments.

It was pure instinct, plus over ten years of being a police officer, that caused me to draw my weapon and fire. I hit him in the shoulder of the arm that held the revolver, which went flying off behind him. He had a shocked look on his face before he fell in a clump on the tracks. I jogged over to him. His childish sobs were not getting me to believe he was approaching death.

"You shot me." There was snot in his nose and phlegm in his throat and piss in his pants.

"Well, you damn fool. You shot at me first."

His wide grin came back slowly at the same time I felt my face go flat. I realized I would have to practically drag this drunk and bleeding fool back to the Municipal Building, find a doctor to patch him up, and file a report. An Epsom salt bath would have to wait.

As bad as my feet were when I ended my workday, my back and shoulders ached more by the time I got my prized possession where he needed to be. The kid was nowhere to be found and would have been useless anyway. Lopez didn't do much to help his own cause by being dead drunk and dead weight. It probably saved him the pain from the bullet wound. Dr. Brenz was available to tend to the wound. Dr. Louis E. Brenz always seemed to be available, from as far back as delivering me, or so I was told. He had a face like a burned up wheat field after a drought but the voice of a dove. He was responsible for bringing half the police force into the world, and never regretted one of them. By the time all the forms were filled out and I handed Lopez off to the jailer, it was pushing midnight.

Dr. Brenz noticed I was limping and passed me a small bottle of spirits of wintergreen. Told me to mix a couple of drops with warm water, take a washcloth and rub my feet with the solution. I thanked him but I had something a little more potent back at my place.

Prohibition didn't go over too well in this part of Kansas, especially being so close to the Oklahoma border and the Cookson Hills where Charles Arthur Floyd grew up. I had read stories in the Arkansas City *Traveler* about Floyd spotted here or Floyd thought to be there, or some such idiocy. No one rightly knew where he was. As for booze, I knew several fellow officers who had access to homemade hooch from backwoods stills either from a distant cousin or a friend of a friend. I wasn't sure that made them bad guys, although I could have pointed a few fingers at the ones that truly were. However, booze from stills didn't work for me. It wasn't that I was against any man taking a drink. I was more concerned my insides might rot away from what they were cooking up. I had seen boys back in the war with devices slapped together from spare parts. I wondered if the rotgut would get us before the Huns.

I got home late but not much later than before. It didn't bother me all that much seeing how I didn't have a family or a girl or anyone else to be tied to. 'Home' was a spacious apartment in Mrs. McGuire's rooming house, one that had a private entrance and its own toilet and bath. She wanted me there as much for her own protection and sense of safety as anything else, although her concerns were puffed up. She may have been seventy-one or -two but she knew the business end of a double-barreled shotgun. It was nice feeling needed. She would have reminded me of my mother if I could have remembered what my mother looked like. You're not supposed to be losing your memory at thirty-six but somehow things kept slipping away. Maybe that was by design.

I splashed a good amount of cold water on my face. It was the only thing to dull the pain from the scars. Fifteen years ago, the doctors said they would fade after one of the first surgeries of its kind. I was still waiting. I looked at the reflection in the mirror, actually stared at it. I couldn't help but do so every time. I always seemed to have a hard time realizing who I was and how I got there. I never imagined my life turning in this direction.

I wasn't up for starting a fire in the potbelly stove so I just poured cold water in the pan I was going to use for my Epsom salt bath. I let five drops of the spirits of wintergreen slip into the water, grabbed a clean towel, and sat on the bed. The scent of the mint rose from my feet to my nostrils and made me think of sweets at Christmas. There was a cool sensation followed slowly by a tide of warmth from my toes to my ankles. I reached into the drawer of my bedside table and pulled out the flask that contained some whiskey I got from a man in Winfield, a local pharmacist who sold whatever he could on the side. He claimed this had come from a doctor in Joplin so I guess that about made it medicinal in spite of what Dr. Brenz might say to the contrary, and a darn sight safer than the local stills. The warmth in my belly equaled the warmth on my feet. I didn't need a blanket that night.

Chapter Two

It was supposed to be my day off but George McAllister had been sick. Chances are he was hungover. Rogelio Lopez wasn't the only person in town to go a little crazy on a Friday night after getting paid. Chief Taylor preferred to have a minimum number of men on patrol to prevent any lapse where trouble might spring up so we could be prepared. Seems he always called on me to fill in seeing how I didn't mind. It was something to do to pass the empty hours.

George often acted like a young version of me, except without the war experience. Too bored to work on a farm all his life and wanting to do something a little more exciting. He had built up his body so he didn't look like a pipsqueak, but he had no concept of death, certainly not the way I witnessed it in the trenches. It was dark and muddy, devoid of dignity, and stank of decay. He probably never thought about getting killed trying to stop a robber. Worse than that would be getting into the middle of a fight between a couple where the husband was madder than a hornet. He didn't think this wasn't a charmed life and he'd have to work every day just to take another breath.

Might have been different if he knew about war like I did. I don't know why they called it the Great War because dirty socks and underwear that didn't get changed often, if at all, and food so far from your mom's home cooking, had nothing great about them. I actually saw the effects of Yperite—what they called mustard gas—on a group of English soldiers: the bulging eyes of the dead staring straight into hell with faces covered with blisters. I can't forget the reddish rust of dried blood on brownish-green uniforms or the caked-on black bile from guts torn open and spilled by bayonets. There was nothing else in the world like it. Maybe it was a world all its own.

I never heard the shell that exploded some fifty yards behind me, never felt a part of my skull chipped away. I could only see a mass of barbed wire coming straight for my face as I fell and wondered if those tiny pieces of metal actually could completely pluck out my eye. A soldier who witnessed the event told me I was like a wild beast caught in a trap, twisting and gyrating so fervently I actually caused more pieces of my face to be ripped away from the bone. Strange thing was I was trying to get away. Maybe I was always trying to get away. Fortunately for him, George McAllister never knew the tortures of the damned. If he was lucky, he never would. I hoped it wouldn't take something tragic for him to learn.

I remember when Charlie Noble got himself an Indian and had the honor of being Arkansas City's first motorcycle cop. They offered me a chance to ride one but I declined. I preferred walking my beat, which is probably why my feet were always bothering me. I liked being around the people I was protecting and keep a watchful eye over them. It was important to look at them and see their faces, look into their eyes, look into their hearts. They thought they could see into mine but they were usually wrong. Most of them were respectful when they looked at me, trying to see beyond the scars and remember the boy that grew up in their midst. I was grateful for that. It made it easier for me because I didn't always remember as well.

Martin Childers was standing outside of Albert's Drug. He was trying too hard to act casual. As owner of Kanotex, one of the refineries in town, and a man known to have a great deal of political influence, it didn't seem natural for a man like that to be loitering outside of the front of a drug store. Knowing his type, he must have had some business to attend to and wouldn't have considered it loitering. With his light brown fedora, gray wool suit, red and white striped bow tie, and a face chiseled out of Kansas limestone, he looked like he was ready to chew gristle off a bone and spit it out cleanly into a pile of dung.

"Howdy, Baron." His affable tone had the undercurrent of the serpent in the Garden of Eden. I wasn't interested in eating no apple.

"Mr. Childers," I responded, tipping my hat.

"Heard you had another run-in with old Lopez last night." The ink on the report was barely dry and here was Childers with more than likely all the particulars. It was not uncommon knowledge a man or two on the force took some extra pay from Martin Childers to make sure he knew what was going on and when.

"Nothin' out of the ordinary."

"Except this time you had to shoot him."

My smile was as easy as a warm summer day. "Well, that might make him think twice the next time payday rolls around."

Childers had an oily smile on his face. He knew I wouldn't be anything but respectful and nothing else.

"What do you think about them folks down in Oklahoma letting Clyde Barrow and his bitch get away? From what I heard, they had near a thousand men scouting them out."

"Well, that'd be their problem, Mr. Childers."

"Until it's ours."

I smiled, tipped my hat again, and then kept moving on. Somehow I got the feeling that if I had more than a minor conversation with Martin Childers my feet would wind up set in stone.

I knew enough about guys like Childers to know what they could do for me and what they could do against me. All of it was just speculation. But when you placed it on the scales, I figured it was best to just mind my own business and move on about my way, trying my best not to ruffle anyone's feathers. I was happy where I was in life. I didn't have the drudgery of working on a farm, yet I did worry for my life. My face was scarred from the war but I wasn't a scary monster like a Halloween creature. Then again, I would look like Clark Gable. There were enough people in town that respected me and even thought I was a hero. There were also a few men like Martin Childers who thought I might be dangerous. At least that was the way it felt.

I could have easily had more money and better clothes and maybe even a car. To gain all that, I would have had to sell off a lot more of my soul than had already been bartered. I was satisfied in knowing I would die here in this quiet, sleepy, boring little town, hopefully at a ripe old age, instead of snuffed out over a few square miles of territory and the so-called loyalty of supposed friends. Somehow it made it better, more acceptable, more honorable. I'd still be dead, but I'd sleep a lot more soundly.

I got down to the farthest end of Fifth Street to the north when I came across Big Ray Vernon. We called him Big Ray because he was well over six-foot-six inches tall, played basketball for the high school, and could have played under Phog Allen at University of Kansas if he could have let go of his momma's apron strings. Instead, he became a lawman, feared by some largely on account of his height. Yet every time I'd seen him for the last several months, he was spooked like the devil on account of Wilbur Underhill getting killed down in Shawnee, Oklahoma. Now, with Clyde Barrow and Bonnie Parker eluding a dragnet of over a thousand police and national guardsmen in the Cookson Hills, the hairs on the back of his neck were standing straight up. Big Ray felt like they were all coming here, to Arkansas City, Kansas, the center of the known world.

"How're you doin', Ray?" I was about as relaxed as I could be.

"On guard, Baron."

"Now, you know that kind of stuff ain't gonna happen here." I knew what he was talking about and I said the same things every time to try and calm his fears. It never worked but I always tried. I figured it might make sense to him one of these days.

"They're all from around here. You know that, don't you, Baron?"

"Underhill weren't. Neither are Clyde Barrow and Bonnie Parker. They're from Texas." He didn't have much of a response but he was still scared nevertheless. It seemed to me the police force was made up largely of farm boys, war veterans, and old-time fools who didn't suffer bandits too gladly. When it came to petty theft, drunkenness, and minor assaults, we were all well equipped to keep the peace. I don't think any of us were prepared to face hardened criminals or desperate gangsters or anyone who just didn't give a damn for their own lives or anyone else's for that matter. It would take something harsh and desperate for our true character to come out.

Chapter Three

The proprietor of the motor court was a short skinny man in his sixties, balding, with drawn-in deep-set eyes that always looked like he'd just woken up. He seemed to have the shakes, like he had a nervous disorder or maybe he was just too cold. Jake knew he was impressed by him, standing upright in a gray suit with deep blue silk shirt and tightly knotted black tie, driving a shiny and relatively new two-door Ford sedan. The twitch of the proprietor's nostrils brought in the fragrance of the perfume that was coming from the elegant woman alongside. He could imagine it was something the man's wife had nagged at him about for years. The driver knew it was strange to be such a well-off city man in these parts. Unfortunately, he had no other choice.

"It's got a real comfy bed, electricity, and a bathtub. I'm sure your wife would want to take a hot bath at the end of a long day." Jake Hickey was thinking the guy could save his spiel. It had already been a stressful drive and it hadn't been half over. They had already decided this was where they were stopping, although if he had any more in him, he'd have kept going. He was not used to driving country roads for long distances. City streets were more his speed.

It was just coming into spring but the evening had a bite to it. Maybe that's all Missouri was. He had never been here before and didn't much like what he saw so far. Other than St. Louis, which he drove right through, it was all a giant forest. Jake preferred city sidewalks and not trees. The crackle of pine needles was not the same as the sound of leather shoes slapping on pavement. He didn't have a notion where he was being sent.

"Gonna need one in the back, away from the road." Hickey had blurted it out, making it sound awkward as the words echoed in his ears. No need to get this old guy all filled with ideas. "Been driving a long time and just want to get some sleep is all. You know?"

"Yes, sir. Number six." The proprietor held out a set of keys, almost on the verge of saluting the dapper man as though he were an officer. Perhaps the old guy wasn't catering to the gentleman as much as he should. "Got a little fried chicken left. It's cold by now, but my missus makes the best around these parts."

"You go ahead and send some over. And anything else you can think of." He pulled a fin out of his pocket and handed it to the man. His eyes grew wider than saucers. That made it a two-dollar tip.

"You'll be staying for breakfast?"

At this point, he was too tired to remain polite. "No." Hickey turned from the man and walked back to the car.

He could see she was sitting uncomfortably, looking out the window, still as bored as when they left Chicago two days ago. He knew, at the time, she had no other options. He knew she wished she had stayed, regardless of the consequences. By and large, he didn't care too much then or now what her attitude was. They still had a way to go, at least another three hundred plus

trusted no one else but Jake. Now, he was returning the favor.

Heather had known hard times until she figured out how to use her body. Then she discovered champagne and bubble baths, and there was no going back to beans and cold showers. Jake knew she would go along with anything because she knew he would take care of her. He could tell she was making sure he knew how disappointed she was.

All the driving was wearing him out and the last thing he needed was some ribbing from a pampered dame who didn't have the good sense to keep her mouth shut. She grabbed the smaller of her suitcases from the floor and started to walk past him, toward the bathroom. He grabbed her arm harshly. She didn't wince or squirm or make a peep.

"Just remember I can drop you off anywhere along the way and it won't matter a thing to me." His hot breath was like a blanket on her face. It smelled of sobriety and the sad thought of an overwhelming sense of responsibility. She yanked her arm out of his grip and leaned even closer.

"You won't."

She turned and strutted toward the bathroom, shaking her ass in a come hither manner, and slammed the door behind her. She was prepared for an invasion that would soak them both. She actually hoped for it. That would be the kind of thing to give her an advantage once again.

Jake knew he didn't love her. More times than naught, she was more trouble than she was worth. At this point though, she was there for cover. A man traveling alone is bound to draw more attention than a

coup   f only he could get her to just shut up and not
ride   This was a tough situation for both of them.
He w   rtain, however, they could get through it if
they j   led their time.

     H   ped for a moment and walked in a tight
circle,   ng around to catch a complete view of the
cabin.   athroom was in a rear corner. Perhaps it
had a w   ; he hadn't seen the room before she went
in. The t   in beds were backed against the far wall.
Lying in   afforded the opportunity to watch the
door. In be   en was a small table with a drawer, a
good place to t a Browning .32 automatic but perhaps
not long enou to hold a Colt .38 Special with a six-
inch barrel.] t would wind up under the pillow.
There was one ndow, just to the right of the door as
you walked in d past the light switch. Heavy dark
green curtains c red it, and Jake made sure they were
shut. Perhaps h vas being overly cautious. He had
only left Chicag couple of days ago, and no one he
knew was aware was gone. He obviously wouldn't
be able to mak s court appearance for firearms
possession. By th a bench warrant would be issued
and he would off y be declared a fugitive. It was
the whole point of to Kansas.

     The place smel arthy, like dirt and wet stone. It
wasn't something h is used to with so little of it
anywhere around hii a city. Sitting comfortably in
his apartment in Chic r at the diner down at the end
of the block where h lly took a breakfast was all
he knew. He couldn ember ever having these
odors in his nostrils b Unlike a lot of poor farm
boys, he had only kno grit and grime of the city
streets. He didn't like l nest these smells were to

him.

She came out wrapped in a towel, hair wet, smelling of talcum and lust. With her back to him, she opened one of her suitcases and pulled out a long sheer negligee. She dropped the towel, and put the nightgown on, stretching her hands high above her head. She turned around to face him highly pleased with herself.

"Well, what do you think?" she offered.

"Nothing I ain't seen before."

She bent over and kissed him forcefully on the lips, allowing her ample cleavage to show. She stood back up and smiled as though she had just done something wrong but didn't really care.

"You smell good," he said with a respectful amount of admiration.

"You want me?"

"Not tonight."

She raised an eyebrow as though to say *Oh, well.* This trip to Kansas was going to continue no matter what she did or said, and slid softly in under the covers.

Chapter Four

I didn't mind the drive up to Winfield all that much except every now and then one of the younger cops chided me over my Ark City roots. High school rivalries didn't interest me much any more, especially all those years removed. I figured it would be a while before these boys saw something of the real world and realized there was a lot more to life than childish pranks.

As I was standing there smiling as big as I could, I realized I must have told the story a million times if it was once. The sweet young clerk behind the counter at the Cowley County Courthouse had these pretty green eyes so it didn't bother me much to tell it a million and one.

"Well, see, my mom named me Byron, you know, after the poet." She nodded as though she had read *She Walks in Beauty* with bated breath. "She had some learning before she met my dad and had some ideas about me being an artist some day. Imagine that." It was the point in my story that I always half smiled and half chuckled. "It was some clerk, probably a heck of lot less pretty than you, who spelled it wrong on the birth certificate."

"So you ain't a real baron?" It seemed like my story went right past her and on over to the next county. This one probably read nothing more taxing than

Photoplay.

"No, ma'am." It felt awkward referring to this little girl by such a respectable title. I understood that was how it was supposed to be done around here, so I followed the proper course of action and maintained my discretion.

When we picked up Will Bell in Ark City for trying to steal a car, we had no idea how much of a record he really had. The chief made a call up to Winfield, and we found out we had an honest-to-goodness thief wanted in three states, who needed to be brought up to Joplin for arraignment. The sheriff's office didn't have anyone available, and our jail wouldn't hold him if any of his friends decided to come on by for a not-quite-cordial visit. I was asked to take him up first thing the next morning. I figured the shackles would be necessary. Little did I think a gag would have been useful.

This was no Pretty Boy Floyd or Wilbur Underhill but he did have a long record of stealing, or trying to steal, just about anything that wasn't nailed down or tied up. He might have had sticky fingers but he was no desperado. Nevertheless, he talked himself up bigger than Dillinger.

"You law ain't got half a notion what I done. It ain't all there in no file. That's just the stuff I let you know about. I got suds stashed all over these here parts and plenty of friends to boot." It went on like that for forty straight minutes, a mastermind and criminal genius with the lung power of a Washington politician, only not as crooked. I should have been honored to be escorting such a rare talent.

I had a notion to visit my merchant friend and see

if he had any of his special medicine available. I finally realized it was no longer able to help me wash away the troubles of constant pain or memories so dark no amount of sunshine could penetrate. The only thing I could do was to keep growing into who I was destined to become and let the past fade away over time. In the reflection of a haberdashery, I saw the scars that were like roadways on a map. The problem was those roads went nowhere.

Unlike Arkansas City where I was a regular everyday fixture, my appearance here caught more people off guard. In spite of my uniform, I felt I was being looked upon with more disgust than someone like Will Bell. This journey was going to continue to get harder until enough time had passed or enough people died. The only thing left for me to do was wait.

The chief told me this was my only task of the day and as soon as Bell was turned over to the county sheriff's office my day was done. I took the opportunity to drive back slowly, weaving my way through some rough county roads and clear my head from worries that had started bothering me again. I figured some of the countryside would remind me of pure simplicity and I could gain a measure of peace. Any effort was worthwhile.

A few miles out of town, I came across a man chopping wood. He looked to be about sixty, white frizzy hair and a day or two's growth of beard. He was wearing a faded pair of overalls with no shirt, and brown boots that seemed to be close to losing their soles. He stopped suddenly when I pulled up, took out a handkerchief from his back pocket to wipe his brow, and screwed up his eyes like he was trying to shut me out.

"Howdy," I said with a friendly tone. He just nodded. "Pretty hot day, huh?" It was small talk, the kind of things you say to fill the empty gaps of uncertainty.

"Suppose so."

His less-than-friendly demeanor was interrupting my desire to have a quiet afternoon. The scowl that was starting to form spoke of a hatred I hadn't seen since the war.

"Look, I'm just passing through. I'm not on the lookout for no one."

"The law's always lookin' out for someone."

Maybe this man had a still somewhere around here or was a relative of Ford Bradshaw. I knew a lot of the folks in these parts didn't realize most of the police were guys that had grown up in the area and knew them and their kin. I understood all about their attitudes and opinions of the government men and the bankers and how they felt those groups were responsible for all the poverty. It just didn't occur to me I was being lumped in with them.

The man wiped his brow again. I noticed his eyes were peering off to the side, toward a clump of trees. Either there was something I wasn't supposed to know about or someone waiting for me to make a move. If I got out of the car, I couldn't be sure what would happen next. I was out of my element, on farmland I wasn't at all familiar with, staring down a man with a sharp axe and skittish eyes. Whoever he was, and whatever he was actually doing, didn't seem all that important now. Maybe good old Charles Arthur Floyd was sitting quietly in those trees waiting to add another lawman to his list of credentials.

"You have a nice day." I drove off, not waiting for a reply and taking a few extra looks back in the rearview mirror. It would have taken nothing for a shotgun blast to come roaring out from those trees, my insides painting the windshield before me, my body hastily buried in a dusty dry field, and my car broken into bits and pieces. There was only one thing I was afraid of, but this surely wasn't it.

You know that any day you could be on the wrong side of a gun, with the finger on the trigger connected to someone who has no interest in your life or your family or your future. You live with this notion because you've chosen to work for the law and in these desperate times, that didn't guarantee you anything. It was just the side you had chosen. It didn't necessarily make it right. I fought against the Germans who didn't speak my language or have any notion of my home. They had their own agenda, which I never knew anything about. It was probably easier to deal with not knowing why someone was out to get you.

I was driving a police vehicle so I had to sign it back in per regulations. I ran into Big Ray just coming on for his shift.

"Hey, I heard you took old Will Bell up to Winfield."

"Yeah." I lowered my voice, and let my gaze land somewhere between my feet and halfway down the road.

"You all right, Baron?"

"I come across a farmer chopping wood about three miles south of Winfield. Acted like he was hiding something."

"Most of them up there are. Still. Moonshine…"

"Think they hide people?"

It was probably a mistake to start up this line of questioning given Ray's queasiness about his job. Unfortunately, I'd opened my yap and now it was time for him to think the Apocalypse was nigh upon us.

"Think Clyde Barrow is back? Maybe Pretty Boy?"

"A little while back, I think it was '32, Floyd was around here a bit. They say he's running with Dillinger now."

"How do you know? Even the government men don't know where they're at."

I'd had a version of this conversation with Big Ray just about every time someone brought up one of the country's more desperate robbers. This time, though, I was starting to appreciate his concerns just a bit more. There'd been talk of some goings on up north and maybe a few rats leaving the sinking ship. Who knew if they'd try to hide out down here? It wouldn't be hard to fit in, making it that much harder to figure out who was who seeing as how no one had to look like who they were. This was something I knew all too well.

Chapter Five

I had hardly stepped through the door the next morning when the chief called me into his office. Chief Taylor stood as tall as Big Ray but his arms seemed like they could wrap around a tractor. One of his hands was big enough to hold a newborn baby. His handlebar moustache looked like it belonged in a gambling hall in San Francisco back in the gay 90's. But his eyes were a cold blue that allowed nothing from the outside to penetrate.

"Officer Witherspoon, I got a call from Sheriff Anders up in Cowley County this morning."

"Was there a problem with the prisoner transfer, sir?" I stood at rigid attention much the way I had in the Army.

"No, he didn't say anything about that." He tugged at his moustache, twisting the end like he was forming a noose. It was a sign many of us had become used to noticing. "He said you were harassing a cousin of his."

It took me a while to figure out what he meant before I realized the hard-working backwoods cracker with the mean face and bad attitude was the offended family member. Perhaps I had indeed intruded upon something, and this man was protected to the extent that a duly appointed county sheriff could throw his weight around. It was no different than anywhere else I suppose. Maybe even right here.

"No, sir. I encountered a gentleman working and passed a brief conversation before departing."

"Perhaps it would be best the next time you make such a trip to come straight back the way you came. Am I making myself clear, Officer Witherspoon?"

"Crystal."

He dismissed me with half of his mouth upturned in a smile that spoke of similar youthful indiscretions. I say that because our job was not to rub anyone the wrong way or run roughshod over fellow officers. There were enough takers for free drinks and pleasantries from ladies that it was foolish to try to sweep the streets clean. Chief Taylor understood the bigger picture, which was to keep the city upright and moving forward, in light of all the more well-known offenders in the area.

I was trying hard to accommodate his notion of propriety when I ran into Councilman Hallett. Literally. My mind had been wandering, and I paid no attention to the man caught up in the latest edition of the *Traveler*. He was standing steps away from the office he still kept as a lawyer. It was an awkward moment but we both recovered as gentlemen tend to do.

Hallett always wore a black bow tie against a starched white shirt and linen pants held up by brown leather suspenders. His straw boater was recognizable from a distance. He looked like a gentleman farmer from the days of the Civil War and did everything he could to perpetuate an image of gallantry. It was a monumental task considering some of his dealings with the more unscrupulous members of the Oklahoma City political gangs. These, of course, were rumors. I thought he allowed them to spread to enhance his reputation. To me, he was just another thief like Will Bell, only better dressed.

"Officer Witherspoon."

"Councilman Hallett."

We both nodded politely.

"I regret your difficulties with Mr. Lopez. Again."

"No problem at all, sir."

"We are all interested in keeping the town as quiet as possible." It was a strange expression to use. Most politicians tend to refer to keeping the town *clean* as though the bad influences make it dirty. I had no idea what alternative forces he may have been referencing nor was it my business to consider. However, just by his comment, I considered a couple of mill workers from around six months ago who acted the same way as Rogelio Lopez. They were blowing off some steam on a payday, got a good talking to, and never acted up again. The problem now was I knew nothing more of them, as though they had simply disappeared from both the mill and the city. I was aware the newspapers said we were still in the middle of a Depression, but it seemed awkward these two were simply gone, as though they were never meant to be here in the first place. Perhaps our location, halfway between Wichita and Oklahoma City, made us nothing more than a stopover for the weary.

Councilman Hallett seemed to be done with his politicking. With a bright white smile that appeared painted on his face, he went on past me with a folded up newspaper tucked under his arm, sauntering as though he didn't have care in the world. As far as I knew, he didn't.

I continued on my patrol, being somewhat nervous

when I walked past Handy's Millinery. I tried my best not to look in for fear of making eye contact with Beth. Elizabeth Handy was the old man's youngest daughter, a good ten years younger than me, and still harboring the crush from when she was a kid and a teenage Baron Witherspoon went off to war. She never looked at the scars and never saw anything other than the young man who treated her with courtesy and respect. Time had changed all our attitudes. She couldn't accept the fact I was a completely different man, and I still saw her as a young schoolgirl who thought the world was a parade.

She was pretty with curly sandy hair and big bright blue eyes that would grab you like a thresher. Her heart could embrace all the joy and pain this cold world could dole out. I knew she couldn't handle the misery my life would lay upon her, and I gave her no reason to think otherwise. Still, she remained as devout as a nun worshipping on the altar of a dead man. It would have been better for her if she just thought of me that way. I had made it about two feet past the open door when I heard her voice echoing like a songbird from inside.

"Oh, Officer Witherspoon."

I stopped dead in my tracks and spun around like I was at a Saturday night dance after a barn-raising. She stood there in the doorway, one eyebrow raised the same way my third grade teacher would when I had done something wrong.

"Yes, ma'am."

"Are you gentleman going to do anything about these young vandals?"

"Which vandals are you referring to, Miss Handy?"

"Those schoolboys that race up and down the sidewalk and bothering folks that are potentially wanting to come into my father's store. Why, they're here about every afternoon after school."

I pulled out my notebook and took down the information she provided, descriptions and times and even some names. After all, I was a duly appointed police officer. Beth did this every so often as a way to be near me for a few moments. She knew I wouldn't allow her to enter my darkness. She thought she would just sprinkle some light on me to wash it away.

I knew why I kept her at a distance. She was too young to realize how cruel the world could be. She was a devoted church-going lady who still believed in the inherent goodness of things. I wouldn't be the one to break the news to her otherwise. I often wondered why I had no desire for some woman to share my pain. Maybe it was the fact that I still felt as though I were hiding and I just wasn't ready to come out. Maybe I never would. So, instead of the wife and the children and the white picket fence and the Sunday gatherings with the neighbors and the vacations to the Ozarks, I opted to keep the bad guys away so others could enjoy these small joys in life. I would have to be content with the happiness of others. I would have to see Beth Handy's happiness from afar.

"I will share this report with my fellow officers, ma'am."

"You do that." Her smile had warmed my heart for as long as I had known her but she knew nothing more would become of this. For that, I felt bad for her and yet relieved as well.

It would have been too easy to take a little from the gravy bowl like I knew others were doing. I could have had a new car or maybe a silk shirt. Then again there was no place I needed to get to and no reason to look so sharp. The mirror showed me all I was and all I needed to be.

Chapter Six

Gripping the wheel as though it were the only thing holding him upright, Jake Hickey was mouthing some kind of sentences, silently reciting a kind of personal rosary. It probably appeared to Heather DeVore he was talking to voices inside his head. The conversation was whispered and not directed at her. He was rehearsing, trying to become a new character, someone who would fit in to this countrified area and not act like a silk suit and a fedora were the most important thing he could buy. He had to behave in such a manner; he was aware there was a Depression going on, and he was trying to get by just like everyone else. He'd have to be as good an actor as James Cagney. Given the situation, it might have been safer to be William Powell.

"This isn't going to work," she said, almost as though she were yawning.

He was brought back to the reality of the long ride, mildly amused by a town called Rolla. The pleasant diversion of his character preparation turned into an annoyed disturbance as the smile melted from his face and a tight-lipped frown took hold.

"If it doesn't, we're both dead. You keep that in mind." Now he knew why he didn't get married and have kids. She was acting like a brat. "And you better put some effort into this, too. We're a couple. Remember?"

As the ride wore on, he watched her try to sleep as the car bounced over rough roads. It was better for the both of them when she had her eyes and mouth closed. He never used to feel this way about her. She was fun to have around in Chicago, a raucous party girl who pushed everything to the edge. She would flirt with the guys, even the married ones, and Jake would laugh it off. The booze was flowing and the North Siders were in charge. But the world was a funny place now and things had to change. He knew she didn't quite accept such a notion. The way she acted, footloose and fancy-free, it was obvious she expected the party to last forever and not fade away into the dirt roads of the Heartland. Jake was already aware how difficult this was going to be and how she was going to be in for a rude awakening if she didn't get with the program fast.

Jake passed the time preparing for a different kind of life. He would have to work, go home and have dinner and do nothing, be the bored kind of guy he always used to make jokes about. He would have to do this for six months, maybe a year, knowing he would come out clean on the other side. It's what George promised so it was easy to think this way. The road ahead of him was rocky with no skyscrapers or speakeasies or hardly any other cars. It was as though he were moving further and further away from anything human and deeper into the blankness of anonymity. He could already sense it for the last several days on this ride, the landscape fading from concrete sidewalks and city lights to gravel and farmland. Everything being stripped away in his view, as though people were an added attraction to the landscape and had no meaning or identity. He hoped it wouldn't happen to him. Pretending to be an Everyman was one thing; becoming a Nothing was unacceptable.

A dip in the road woke her harshly. Her head bobbed and a few strands of her finely coiffed hair hung in her face. She shifted around, obviously uncomfortable from the hours of riding in this car. She tried to stretch like a cat but there was no place to go.

"I'm hungry," she moaned.

For the first time since they left Chicago, he agreed with her on something.

There were two tractors and a flatbed pickup truck parked in front of Mae Belle's Diner. A bright red Coca-Cola sign was about the only color on the white clapboard building. The hinge on the screen door was loose and slammed shut as they entered. There was a short counter just as they walked in with all five stools occupied by men in overalls, with various colored handkerchiefs or cloths sticking out of their back pockets. It seemed as though each of them had years of grit under their fingernails. Just to the left, were two booths with red Bakelite tabletops. In the middle was a small table with two chairs.

Maybe she thought her wavy hair made her look like Fay Wray, but with her freckles the waitress looked more like Shirley Temple. The embroidered nametag read SHEILA. Jake wondered who Mae Belle was.

"You folks look plain tuckered out," Sheila said cheerily as though she had never been tuckered out herself. "Where you headed?"

At first, Jake's naturally suspicious city nature took over. He relaxed and tried to act as laid back as possible. "Winfield. Kansas. My cousin's got a job for me. Got to go where the money is, you know?"

Shelia looked at their clothes and caught a glimpse of their car outside. There as a knowing smirk on her face, not too impolite yet hopeful of a decent tip.

"Special today is meatloaf, mashed potatoes, and gravy." The lilt was apparent in her voice.

Heather had opened her mouth before Jake practically blurted, "Sounds great."

They ate in silence with Jake shoveling his food in as fast as he could. Maybe he was trying to eat quickly and continue on or maybe he really was that hungry and the food might have been halfway decent after all.

Heather cut her meatloaf with a knife as though she were dining on filet mignon. A little imagination could go a long way toward turning a nothing into a something. Jake was pleased she could remain both silent and dignified. He smiled at her a couple of times. It was more like the pleasant smirk of a husband who had won a bet with his wife. The issue was, they weren't married. She looked at him with one eyebrow raised, nodding ever so slightly. It was all a game that needed to be played.

Jake decided it would be best if he didn't have to wait on Sheila to bring them their tab. He stepped up to the counter and stood alongside what appeared to be a local farmer. The overalls were grimy and worn. The flannel shirt appeared almost frayed through at the elbows. The growth of beard could have scrubbed a pot clean. Jake's gaze met the old codger. He nodded politely.

"They got work in Kansas?"

At first, Jake wasn't sure the man was talking to him, then he remembered the earlier conversation with the waitress.

"Yes, sir."

"What kind of work?"

"Machine shop." Jake figured that was general enough to answer a variety of questions.

"Good with your hands, are ya?"

It was everything he could do to prevent a broad smile from being plastered on his face like a billboard. "Yes, sir." It galled him to have to call this hayseed *sir* but he was proud of the restraint he was showing.

The old man turned in his seat and took a long look at Heather. She was dusting her face with the mother-of-pearl compact, perhaps not appearing as desperate as she needed to given their cover story.

"Long way to Kansas. You best be careful on the roads."

"Oh?"

"Got a lot of city folk passing through this way all the time."

"Is that a bad thing?" Jake asked, naively.

"When that city is Chicago it is."

He didn't care if the two dollar bills were an extreme tip. He needed to leave with Heather right then. His thought the notion of a big city boy coming down to hide among the stiffs and hicks and backwoods crackers had come undone. These folks were smarter than they appeared, and a lot smarter than they would ever let on. Who knows if this good old boy hadn't already seen right through him just as long as there was no one from up North who knew where they were? Then again, an ample enough amount of cash would be just the thing to get these God-fearing church-going bumpkins to turn the way of the devil himself.

He drove faster than he had done before. This time

he muttered to himself, talking like the tough Mick who wouldn't take a nasty look from anyone. Out of the corner of his eye, he caught Heather looking at him with concern, realizing he wasn't pretending to be some countrified Beau Brummell but was actually starting to be concerned. She reached over to him. He sensed her and pulled his arm away. He was no different now than he was when he was around George Moran. This wasn't the best scenario for her either.

"What is it?" The words came out strained, as though there were tears buried in the back of her throat.

"You were right. This won't work. Most of these people know about us. Our kind."

"What do we do?"

He pulled the car to the side of the road, looked around to make sure there was no one nearby. He turned off the engine and swiveled in the seat toward her. "We play this out. We find friends or anyone who can help us in any way. We stay away from any person that seems like they're not on our side. Anyone with an Italian name. Any cops. Any politicians. Any high falutin' businessmen. Just our people. And I guarantee you, there ain't gonna be a whole helluva lot of 'em. They're the ones who'll know how to get us fixed up right."

He didn't like hearing his own words, admitting to defeat before the thing even got started. The worse part was being caught between a rock and a hard place. Chicago was too hot right now, according to Moran. This part of the country was so different from what they were used to they couldn't help but stick out. There was the possibility of doubling back to St. Louis but he had no connections there. Others from the Windy City had come down here when troubles came up. If they could make it, so could he. He just didn't like how it was starting out and realized they were in the lion's den.

"What does that leave us, Jake?"

He looked at her, disgusted by the fact he had let her worm her way into his life. Sure, there were the parties and the laughter and the sex. When it got down to it, she was all he had to rely on in a tough situation. He knew what kind of skills and talent she had; he'd seen it and experienced it. He just couldn't be sure it was enough. Now, she was all he had.

"Only us, kid. Only us."

Chapter Seven

There was something less rural about Winfield, Kansas. Outside of St. Louis, it was the biggest burg they had pulled through in terms of buildings and people milling about. Not that it could match the skyscrapers of the Windy City, but at the vey least the Cowley County Court House had a stylishness to it they hadn't encountered for several hundred miles. On the other hand, it did bother Jake the most elegant thing they had seen in days was a place he never wanted to spend any time in at all.

He figured Heather might be thinking about a marriage license and a Justice of the Peace. As far as he was concerned, most women, even her type, eventually wanted that kind of life: the house with the white picket fence and a chicken dinner on Sunday with a couple of little ones scurrying around at your feet. Maybe she was different. Maybe she would get as bored with the notion as he had been. Then again, Dion O'Banion was a happily married man and a good Catholic, and Capone had a wife and kid. Anything was possible.

The man they were supposed to see was named Twomey and he ran a garage. George never told him exactly where it was located before they had to make tracks out of town. Jake spent close to forty-five minutes driving around and pulling in to every service station he could find. Finally, the man who came out to fill their tank at the umpteenth place looked like he had been expecting them. He was in his mid fifties, gaunt with drawn eyes like a bloodhound, seemingly tired even though he bounced on his feet. He had on a gray work shirt and black pants. He certainly didn't look like one of those boys they had working for the big companies.

"Need a fill?" the man asked.

"Looking for a man named Twomey." Jake was direct, almost bored by asking, and definitely not concerned with hiding his interests any more.

"Keep your voice down." The man was just as direct. "Pull around back. Behind the building." His demeanor transformed from friendly serviceman to hardened drill sergeant. The ease of having all the time in the world evaporated into the precision of a machine. Jake didn't waste a moment following the man's instructions.

A clump of trees that fronted a field was enough of a backdrop to provide cover. Jake's first instinct was to step out of the car but he soon realized he was placing his safety into this stranger's hands and it would be better to just do as he was told. The man came to the driver's side, placed his foot on the running board, and leaned in through the open window.

"They call me Joshua Rackler down here. I was John Twomey in Chicago." It was all recited like a script. There had probably been countless hotheads who had been sent down to this neck of the woods to cool off. At this point, it was no longer a compassionate gesture but an assembly line for gangsters.

"George said you could fix me up with a job and a place for about six months."

"Not here. Down in Ark City."

Days driving on rural roads, not seeing anything that resembled the city life he was used to and regrettably had to give up, he sat there in the car as his eyes started to get wide, feeling the blood flow in straight to his face. He was getting bounced around and just wanted the spinning to stop.

"What the hell is Ark City?"

"Arkansas City," Twomey explained. "Less than fifteen miles south of here."

"I've come all the way from Chicago. I was told to go to Winfield, Kansas and look for Twomey who ran a service station. They said he could fix me up with a job and a scatter for six months. What the hell are you telling me now?"

Twomey was neither apologetic nor sympathetic. He was the man to see down in these parts. He was the only man to see. All he could do, all he was willing to do, was explain the situation as best as he could. His voice was measured and deep and never veered away from the message.

"This town's all full up with your type."

Jake decided not to take offense to the comment, recognizing he and Heather were different from these folks.

"Got a man runs a packing company. Also owns some apartments and a hotel. The pay is good. The rent is cheap. Best part is nobody asks you nothing."

Jake knew a job was lined up but never expected to be working in a packing company or any other place that required excessive labor. He sure wasn't prepared to live in an apartment the size of a flophouse, especially when some other hideouts had been nice houses in the Chicago suburbs. Mostly he just never considered how difficult this whole process was going to turn out. After all the days and all the miles, he didn't want to be told he was not at his final destination.

"Do you know who I am? Do you know who sent me?"

Without a second thought, Twomey responded, "You're another punk Mick who set the world on fire and now it's trying to burn you to the ground. This is how it works, buddy boy. You want sanctuary, you got to pay the piper."

Jake didn't look at Heather. This ordeal was turning into a trauma, and he didn't want to deal with anything she might have to say or wind up looking like a weak fool in front of her. He looked down into his lap, trying to think of an alternative to just following instructions like a sheep. When he realized the odds were stacked against him, he looked back at Twomey, and said, "All right. What do we do from here?"

Twomey gave Jake explicit directions on how to get out of town, where to go and how far, and when to turn off to get to the Keefe and LeStourgeon Packing Company. Was told to ask for Giuseppe Gallo. The hair on the back of his neck stood up. He was supposed to seek help from an Italian.

"I know what you're thinking," Twomey blurted, as though he were psychic. "He ain't a guinea like Capone and them. His family's been over since the days of Garibaldi. He don't know nothin' from South Siders."

Jake didn't like it one bit. The thing he told Heather, the one thing that would save them, was to stay away from anyone who could turn against them.

The Italians were even more significant than the police. He couldn't stomach the fact his very life was in the hands of a dago wop.

George had given up on him, sent him down here to this lonely part of the country to get him out of the way, let him fend for himself, maybe come out of it, maybe not. There were too many thoughts swirling around in his head, and he needed to keep clear to focus on the one thing that mattered to him: his life. He wound up accepting all Twomey's information and planned to proceed as instructed, knowing he could alter the plan as soon as something better came along.

"I'm gonna need bullets for a heater," Jake said, as though he were ordering a hamburger.

"Not a good idea carrying iron. The coppers down there are pretty straight when they're not being crooked. Not like in your neck of the woods. You knew they were all on the take. You can't tell a straight from a partner."

"I'm hearing you. Just make me feel more comfortable knowing I can take care of myself"—he paused and shot his thumb in Heather's direction—"and her in a pinch. I've got a bigger picture to look at here. Know what I mean?" Jake schmoozed him to make Twomey feel like he was on the spot. The big brave Mick from Chicago was looking after a frail. Twomey reluctantly told him about a man just a few miles out of town that had been known to help out in those kinds of situations. He needed to stay out of the mix on account of the clean reputation he had acquired. At this point, Jake was done with Twomey. It was on to Arkansas City and the packing company with an employee named Giuseppe Gallo. But first there would be a stop to see a man.

It wasn't especially that hot of a day but the old gent with the frizzled white hair and rough beard was sweating as though it were August. He had on overalls with no shirt and worn brown shoes. He kept chopping logs, making small ones from big ones. Jake stopped the car some thirty feet from him. He didn't say anything, just patiently waited. The man turned, looked at the car and then at Jake and finally at Heather. He pulled a red hanky from his back pocket, wiped it on top of his head and across his face, and then tucked it away. Jake stepped out of the car slowly and walked easily over to the man, his hands out of his pockets and in plain view at all times. He stood in front of the man but gave a good three feet of space between them.

"Don't suppose you know where a man can lay his hands on some bullets for a roscoe?" Jake made sure to never look away from the man's eyes. He slowly reached into his pants pocket with one hand, pulling out a Michigan bank roll.

"What'cha got?"

"Thirty-two Browning and a .38 Colt."

"Browning an auto or semi?"

"Auto."

The old man turned and walked back to his wood. Jake had no idea what he was up to. He thought he had just made a business proposition yet now it appeared the old guy was simply walking away. It was when the guy turned over a wooden case and returned with two boxes of bullets Jake knew he was at the right place. The old guy nodded slightly and Jake took it as a sign to show his green. He removed the rubber band and spread the bills fan style. The old guy took two twenty-dollar bills, stuffed them in his pocket, handed Jake the two boxes, and returned to chopping wood.

This supply wasn't enough to get him out of a serious jam if one came down the pike but it was plenty to ward off any nosey neighbors and two-bit shams. It also told him where there was a friend if needed. He was starting to wonder if it wasn't better had he just stuck it out in the city and took whatever heat came his way. On the other hand, he trusted George and knew better than to think too much. It was easy to feel that way now especially with the extra bullets in tow.

Jake remembered Twomey's instructions and continued on toward Arkansas City.

Chapter Eight

I had heard some rumors that a guy working at the Kanotex refinery wasn't what he appeared to be. The guys at the station passed stories back and forth like old ladies at a quilting bee. Sometimes they made sense. After a sketchy description, I had seen him once or twice around town, shopping for groceries and such, and he seemed amiable. There was something about him, maybe his style or demeanor, which didn't gel with his story of being an oil worker in Texas who got laid off and lost his family because of it.

I passed him coming out of Daisy Mae's. "Howdy," he said with no trace of an accent. He had sandy blonde hair with mean blue eyes.

"Hot day," I mentioned.

"Yes, it is."

"Used to it?"

"Never have been." He smiled and walked off.

The biggest thing I noticed was his hands. They weren't rough or worn or calloused. He looked like he was used to getting a manicure on a regular basis. It was nothing anyone around these parts would even consider.

He was never involved in anything that brought me into the picture as a law enforcement officer so I had no cause to question him. As far as I was concerned, he was an honest citizen. Nevertheless, it got under my skin that there was something not right about him, that he didn't fit in, and that there was a lot more to him than it appeared. After a while, I just didn't see him any more. No one I encountered ever mentioned him or referenced him.

I had to let it go, knowing there were probably a few who felt the same way about me after the war. I came back with a scarred face and a different attitude. I'm certain many people, especially Doctie Brenz, were concerned they weren't getting back the same guy who went off to fight the Huns. Eventually, over time, I was the one they came to accept.

What bothered me the most was all the talk of the Magnolia Ranch, not too far from us, and about ten miles southeast of Winfield. It was built by an old Union general after the war and was impressive enough as a home. There were subtle whispers that "the Grandfather on the hill runs the town" and I knew what it meant. There was an unknown presence running everything around that had no name or identity. It was the real definition of power. I understood how a few men with money and influence could control a town or a city and do with it what they pleased. Ask anyone who's been to Chicago about a town called Cicero. I didn't want Ark City to end up like that. There was a time about ten years ago when the mayor gave Chief Higgins the instructions to make whatever decisions were necessary to clean up the force. It was right around the time I worked the Farmers State Bank robbery in '25. What I remember most about Higgins were his round droopy eyes that made him appear laid back and easy going. He might have been that way at home or in church but when it came around to fighting crime, the man was unstoppable. I was a lot prouder back then. Perhaps I might have even bought into the notion I was a hero. Over the years, I've seen a lot more, mostly from my side of the fence. You get to a point where it takes too much effort to fight every little battle because you know you're not going to win them all.

A shiny black Ford two-door drove slowly down the street. It looked newer, maybe a '32. It's hard to say for sure because I haven't seen a brand new car in a while, at least not since Mr. Childers showed off his 1928 Lincoln at the first Arkalalah. I couldn't see the driver or his passenger on account of the sun glaring off the windows. My interest was based on whether they were passing through town or stopping.

The car pulled over to the far side of the street and the driver called out to a young boy passing by. He rolled the window down and the boy, being rather small, had to stand on the running board to talk to the driver. The kid used his finger to point in one direction and then another, nodding as the man kept questioning him. He handed the boy a coin and then drove off. I looked around and no one else seemed to have noticed the car quite the way I did. I walked slowly in its direction, knowing I wouldn't catch up to it but still wanting to be aware of what was happening.

There was really nothing out of place if a policeman was walking his beat or checking various locations that might have been a festering ground for trouble. A couple of older ladies called out to me, and I tipped my hat as politely as possible. A man in his mid-fifties with a torn flannel shirt and corduroy pants worn at knees turned in the opposite direction when he saw me coming. He was obviously drunk, and I could have easily run him in. That would have taken up more time and pulled me away from my ever-growing curiosity of the shiny black car.

I had walked a good way out of town before the sun glared off the car parked outside the Keefe and LeStourgeon plant. That only made me ask more questions. It might have been a businessman from Wichita, Kansas City, or Oklahoma City. A possible investor or buyer, although I hadn't heard of any financial issues despite the Depression going on. I tried to be as casual as possible walking up to the car. The hair on the back of my neck rose when I saw a license plate from Illinois.

There was nothing illegal about that, per se. But a shiny new black car from that area made you think of gangsters mighty quick. It seems Big Ray was rubbing off on me a bit. It didn't feel right reporting it to Chief Taylor. He did advocate being vigilant in all areas, taking notice of items and events that seemed unusual or out of the ordinary. He also didn't want anyone to go flying off the handle and assuming we were being invaded by a Biblical pestilence. I made it my business to make a mental note of the car and its possible appearance over the next couple of days.

After a day off, my walking beat on Saturday afternoon brought me up to Summit and Fifth, to the Gladstone Hotel. The shiny black Ford was parked out front, just steps away from the front door. I knew one of the front desk men, Phil Garmes. He was as close to being a criminal as you could get without breaking any laws. As an employee at the best hotel in town, I had heard rumors Phil claimed he could get any guest any thing they wanted. It might have been true or it might have been talk. He wore his sandy blond hair slicked down and parted in the middle. His pencil thin moustache hardly showed on account of the light color of his hair but he maintained it on account of the movie stars he had seen. He looked like a Scandinavian version of Valentino with a tenth of the charm.

"Baron," he said with a bold voice upon seeing me. "Or rather, Officer Witherspoon. I can assure you no crimes have been committed here, sir." His attempt at humorous conversation bordered on sarcasm.

"At least not yet." My response was as humorous as his. He gave up the attempt and went back to working on the crossword puzzle in the *Traveler*. It was then Elizabeth Handy walked in with what appeared to be a hatbox. She looked to me, then Phil, then back to me with a coy smile that made her seem like Myrna Loy.

"Good day, gentlemen." I knew she wasn't all that keen on Phil Garmes, even told me what she thought of him in quiet, almost un-lady-like terms. She was showing me how gracious she could be. I was worried she might get in the way of my inquiries.

"The lady's been expecting that." Phil sounded like a supervisor or agent.

"Okay if I go on up?"

"The man said he didn't want to be disturbed."

Elizabeth placed the box gingerly on the counter. "Don't be shaking that all around when you deliver it. It's delicate." She turned quickly from Phil, looked at me as her smile grew, and then flew out of the door like a gust of wind. In spite of the reason for me being there, I couldn't help but smile to myself.

"Looks like you've got a swell staying here."

He was confused at first until my thumb referencing the car out front and nodding my head toward the hatbox clarified my meaning. "For a while."

"How do you mean?"

He leaned in close as though we were planning a meeting of the Anti Horse Thief Association.

"Poor sap from up north got wiped out in a financial scam. Had to come down here for a job at Keefe. All high-fallutin' with a ritzy wife to boot. They're not gonna like it here much."

The shiny new Ford from Illinois got a job down here. I suppose it might have made sense if only for the fact I knew half a dozen guys who got turned down for a job at Keefe and LeStourgeon within the last month on account of there being no more jobs available. Maybe from this so-called financial dealing he had some connections, knew someone who knew someone. I know that kind of thing happens all the time in the big cities. It seemed to me, however, that a man of such distinction wouldn't simply give up so easy and fall all the way down to the bottom of the ladder, especially if he had a wife as hoity-toity as Phil described. Then again, you don't know what people are capable of until they're facing their demons.

"Good for him. I hope he does well." I didn't want Phil to think I had any specific interest in this man as he would have used that knowledge to make sure an extra dollar or two got slapped in his hand. I tapped the front counter, nodded and walked off like I didn't have a care in the world. I was hoping I didn't.

I passed Dr. Brenz coming out of the municipal building as I was checking out from my shift. He seemed to be in a bit of a rush and was flushed and sweating. My comment of "Hey, Doc" startled him to a stop. He did everything he could to hide his nervousness.

"I'm sorry, Baron. I didn't see you."

"Yeah, well, has the chief got you in on a consultation again?"

"What? Oh, yes. A consultation. Yes." Dr. Brenz didn't seem to want to have a conversation but I couldn't figure out what had spooked him.

"You haven't forgotten my physical next week, have you?" Ever since the war and my surgery, Dr. Brenz wanted to give me the once-over every six months. As a boy, Louis Brenz delivered newspapers to Dr. Andrew Still, the father of osteopathic medicine, in his hometown of Kirksville, Missouri. Despite his parents' desire for him to be a schoolteacher, the calling to go into osteopathy was just too great. When I returned back from the war, we discussed my condition in detail. This was well before I joined the police department. He just didn't feel all that comfortable with the work done in France even though some really good doctors had performed it. He also told me he wanted to check me out, psychologically speaking, regarding any traumas relating to the war. I was really intent on letting that part go, knowing that if there were any issues there was nothing he could really do about them, in spite of his confidence in craniosacral therapy. He tried explaining it to me on more than one occasion. I was okay with him knowing its meaning more than me.

"Yes. Certainly. Come by at the usual time. If you'll excuse me."

He turned and walked off as though being chased

by ghosts. If anyone should be walking that way, it probably should have been me.

Chapter Nine

I had agreed to go fishing with Big Ray even though I hated it. He had always seemed like a little brother to me, the kind of guy who is smart and strong and good-natured but has no sense of what the real world is like. I had "been to France" as the saying went and was happy to stay on the farm, so to speak. I truly wanted to provide guidance to the many younger guys on the force but it felt awkward talking about things I really had no business discussing.

There was a cool breeze in the air, surprising for a late May afternoon. I closed my eyes and let it wash over me. I had made up for many of my transgressions of the past and felt as though I could move on. When I tried to think of what to do next, there was only an empty hole in my mind. All I could see was the fog of the mustard gas and the sharp strangulation of barbed wire and the man I called my dearest friend, the one who could not judge me no matter what I had been in the past.

I let Ray keep all the fish we caught. I hated gutting and cleaning the poor bastards and I hated cooking them. As we were heading back, Bobby Hurley, the newest recruit on the force, came running down the street toward us, jumping up and down like a jack-in-the-box.

"They got 'em. They got 'em!" he kept yelling.

"Who?" I yelled back.

"Clyde Barrow and his bitch." He didn't seem to care there might have been ladies in the street.

"They caught 'em?" Big Ray yelled back.

"Nah. Shot 'em up. They're dead."

"Where?" I was now standing in front of him, talking as though we were in the station house and trying my best to keep him from losing any semblance of respectability he might have had.

"Down in Louisiana. Guys had been tracking them. Got 'em in an ambush. Shot the living hell out of 'em. They're dead." Hurley had a big grin on his face as though his frog won the championship jumping contest. He was too new to realize what any of these men had at stake and just how dangerous Clyde Barrow and Bonnie Parker had been. The thing that worried me the most was all these younger kids had no idea what death was and had absolutely no fear. To some, that was a good thing that equated to bravery. If you've ever looked Death in the face, you realize you might not get a second chance. If you do, you savor every little thing in your life like they're the most precious things in the world. Most folks knew my story. I just couldn't let on how much they didn't know.

Intuitively, I stopped by Chief Taylor's office. He knew I wouldn't respond like Bobby or Big Ray. I always felt he could read me, see through me, perhaps even inside me. He never talked about grooming me for detective or anything specifically like that. He just knew I would give him a straight answer. Within reason, of course.

"You heard?" he said, bluntly.

"Yes, sir."

"What do you make of it?"

"Seems like those boys in Louisiana took the fight to them."

"Wasn't any bayou cops. A posse of Texas Rangers. Main guy name of Hamer been tracking them for a couple of months."

"Okay. Texas Rangers then. Probably better equipped in a gun battle anyway."

The chief stood up and came around to the front of the desk, sitting on the edge. He seemed to tower over me, like a bald eagle with its wings spread wide, covering me in shadows.

"They set a trap for them. Pure and simple. Didn't wait to start a gun battle. It was more like an execution. Sad state of affairs, if you ask me. We're sure as heck not prepared for anything like that here."

I wasn't sure why he was telling me this and I didn't know what to say. I had read all about this couple and knew they were like rabid dogs. Any farmer knew what to do with such an animal and that was to shoot it in the head and put it out of its misery. It made no sense to get into any sort of philosophical discussion with the chief because I would have had nothing to gain.

"I remember when I was growing up…" His tone changed to something like Roosevelt on a fireside chat. "Small town outside of Joplin called Tipton Ford. Ever heard of it?" I nodded in the negative, feeling like he wanted to just continue. "Apparently there was this petty thief rummaging through town. Grabbed a shirt from a clothesline or a hammer setting against an anvil. When you added up everything he took, it didn't amount to much. Figured he was just poor and needed those things. Sheriff finally caught him stealing a pie, of all things, cooling on a windowsill. Man's name was Prendergast. Don't recall his Christian name. Anyway, the sheriff took him to each home that got robbed and made him apologize. Each person accepted the apology and that was that. This Prendergast wasn't malicious or mean-spirited and he certainly wasn't evil like those two down in Louisiana. I suppose there are different kinds of crooks out there and some of them deserve a second chance."

Chief Taylor strode back behind his desk and sat down, looking over some folders. He wasn't going to dismiss me like they would in the Army. I just knew he was done. Before I left, I asked, "Whatever became of this Prendergast fellow?"

"He was working for the Missouri and Northern Arkansas Railroad when he got killed in '14. Collision with another train." I hoped he found redemption before that happened.

The world was changing. I sensed it. The Eighteenth Amendment to the Constitution had been repealed by the Twenty-First Amendment although here in Kansas we lagged behind the rest of the country in recognizing that. Capone was in jail on tax evasion, as the Feds had nothing else they could get him on. Now, Bonnie and Clyde were target practice for a bunch of hopped-up hicks from Texas with bad moustaches and worse attitudes. The dominoes were starting to fall in place and it was looking like I might be able to move on with my life and live quietly until I was placed in a pine box. Barely two months later, another bad man went down. It occurred to me maybe the dust was about to get kicked up a bit.

Chapter Ten

It had been just about a year since Jake and Heather made their way down from Chicago to this backwoods Kansas town that tried to make itself out to be part of the big time. He didn't expect to have any difficulty with the Kansas winter. Coming from Chicago, he was used to wearing a wool coat, leather gloves, and a muffler, the notion of pulling up your collar and sinking within your clothes. He had felt the blasts from Lake Michigan cut through him like he was Swiss cheese. He had known what it was like to not be able to feel your nose and the only thing that could warm you up was some of the stolen Canadian whiskey. Kansas was a land of wheat fields and hick farmers and maybe (from what he heard) tornados.

However, the wind blew strong and fast and carried with it a coldness like the chill of death. He would scurry from his car into the factory and out again. During the winter months, he wouldn't leave the building at all. Meanwhile, Heather Devore stayed in the hotel at all times. She listened to the radio. She declined to have Jake take her anywhere for dinner, ordering room service for every meal. She may have been from Chicago as well but she would have preferred to hole up in Miami. She made casual comments how the white sand beaches and warm Atlantic waters would have been more of a sweet touch against her skin than Jake's now hard and calloused hands. He recognized he had turned into a "working man." Suffice it to say neither one of them was anticipating the months of ice nor snow and both were happy when it finally passed.

Jake was growing frustrated at not getting any response to his telegrams to George. For every twenty he'd send, he might get back one response. It was usually the same:

HANG IN THERE. STOP.
HEAT'S STILL ON. STOP.
SAFER WHERE YOU ARE. END.

Jake knew all that. What he didn't know was for how long and when he could come back and what kind of a situation he would be coming back to. He was told six months, maybe a year. Well, the year had come and gone and he might just as well have been on a deserted island. The newspaper told the story in early December of 1933 when Utah became the thirty-sixth state to ratify the Twenty-First Amendment and Prohibition was officially and legally over. Selling booze would be the right of every Joe Citizen and the mob would no longer have a monopoly. They still had the bawdy houses and the numbers but it just seemed like there was no way to keep control and make the money they had been making before. Having a few politicians in your pocket made for ease of passing through ideal legislation. The question now would be what was considered ideal.

The flowers popping up in beds around various homes gave way to the heat of the summer. Then the July 23, 1934 edition of the *Traveler* boldly proclaimed:

Dillinger Slain In Chicago
Shot Dead by Federal Men In Front Of Movie Theater

That changed everything. Capone in prison. Prohibition repealed. Now, the Feds had vigorously gone after and killed John Dillinger, the classiest and smartest bank robber of them all. Jake figured the mob fingered him since all those old-time bandits were interfering with the progress of the syndicates. But what kind of heat were they bringing on themselves by doing so?

It felt bad. He suddenly felt empty and alone, working in a factory in a Podunk town in Kansas with a hottie who wanted action and no real friends to help him climb back up on top. He started looking at everyone around him, figuring there had to be a few other Northern guys around, someone like him, not exactly like him but at least in the same position, trying to blend in and hide and be square until it was safe to go back. Heck, even a Wop would have made good company by now. Then it dawned on him some of the guys who had come down before him might grow used to this kind of life, decide they didn't want to be killed just because they were Irish toughs looking to fatten their bankroll, figuring a decent job and a square meal beat out action and almost certain death. Or worse yet, a heartland hoosegow. That would never happen to him. He knew it for sure. Heather Devore would make sure of it.

"So, they got Dillinger. So what. What difference does that make to you?" All she could see was that Prohibition was over and the bad guy was gunned down. She had no idea how that would affect business.

"Shut up. I'm thinking." It was all he could do. He

was trapped by not knowing what decision others who were in control were going to make. Unless he could be the one in control.

"What's going on with you?"

He turned to her sharply, eyes wild like a Baptist preacher about ready to condemn her sinful ways to eternal hell. "You don't like it here, do you?"

"No." The spitefulness was propelled out of her mouth like bullets from a tommy gun and then seemed to go flat like a shot up tire.

"What if I told you we couldn't go back to Chicago? Ever." She started to respond, even opened her mouth a bit, but it simply stayed open without any words coming out. There was fear in her eyes that melted into hopelessness. Neither of them considered that thought, never figured this would be anything other than a six to nine month annoyance, almost like doing time in Joliet. It was well past that sentence, and they were stuck with each other, unless Jake had an idea for something better.

"This place ain't what it seems. Hicks and farmers and good old boys on the surface. I wasn't the first one George ever sent down here. There's gotta be more of us here. And more of us means we can put a gang together. That means money."

"And where do I get to spend all this money, supposing you are able to put something together? I don't exactly see any nightclubs around."

She had a point. His problem was he never thought like her. She was good to have around to show off and have drinks with and get naked. What she did for entertainment or to occupy her mind never much concerned him. He pulled a wad of cash from his

61

pocket, fanned out the bills, then softly dropped them on the bed.

"That's two hundred dollars. You can take it and go anywhere you want."

She looked down at the cabbage as it glistened in her eyes. It might as well have been dirty bath water going down the drain. It wouldn't last long. She wouldn't be able to figure out how far that would take her. "This is not what I signed up for, Jake."

He moved in closer, placing one hand at the small of her back and the other on her ass, drawing her close, shooting darts into her eyes. "I know, baby. Right now, I'm the best thing in town and I happen to be all yours."

She spent the evening showing her gratitude. Jake couldn't have figured she would be keeping her eyes open for a ticket out.

Chapter Eleven

If it weren't for the headaches, I wouldn't have been back in Dr. Brenz's office. The pain was getting to be more difficult to deal with. Pinpoint, like an ice pick, just above my right eye, like someone was trying to put me out of my misery. Sometimes dizziness or fuzzy colored lines swirling around. I hadn't had them before, not that I could remember. I did suffer headaches years ago when I came back but that was on account of the surgery and the trauma. The doctors back in England said it might happen but didn't really have any idea what to do about them. These headaches didn't start happening until after my last check-up. It was about the time I kept seeing that dandy from the hotel more and more around the city.

Something made me think I knew him but that would have been impossible according to the doc and Chief Taylor. How could a farm boy from Kansas know a tough guy from Chicago? I don't know what made me think of him as a tough guy because I hadn't spoken to him or gotten any sense of him other than what little I had seen. He just looked familiar. Then again, there were many instances where my memory had been jumbled up so that everyone looked familiar. Other times I wasn't able to determine if someone was real or an illusion. It wasn't the kind of thing I discussed with anyone. I had earned a measure of trust and respect. It wouldn't do to have people start questioning my sanity.

Dr. Brenz kept shining the light in and out of my eyes, pulling my eyelids up and down trying to figure out what demon may have gotten into my head. He looked in my ears and nose and down my throat. I was about to gag on the tongue depressor.

"Are you still having the dreams?" he asked while poking at me.

The hero in me responded "No" just a little too quickly.

Doctie stood up and leaned back, taking a couple of steps away and looking at me with a disapproving face.

"Tell me about them."

I exhaled slightly, like a kid who got caught taking his dad's shotgun without permission to go hunting. If you visit the doctor, don't expect him not to know what's going on with you. I always wondered how much he actually knew.

"It's like I'm still in London or something. There's always a fog. Whatever I see, nothing's clear. No details or anything."

"What can you see?"

"Funny thing is I see me. Before the war. Before the injury. My face is, well, like it used to be. And I'm laughing at me. Well, you know, the me I am now. What I've become." I heard myself and wondered if Dr. Brenz thought I was as crazy as I sounded.

"And what have you become, Baron?"

That's when it hit me I was at a crossroads in my life, and I could never discuss it with anyone. I'd have to live with this uncertainty until it either worked itself out or drove me completely off the wagon. How was I going to explain to him that every time I looked in the mirror I didn't know who I was, and it had nothing to do with the injury and the surgery? In order to work toward getting my life more settled, I'd have to tell him everything. All that would have done is kicked up a dust cloud that would have people scratching their heads wondering how they let a bad man into their midst.

My thoughts went back to the guy at the Gladstone. The fancy car. The swanky woman. He didn't fit here, didn't even try to fit in. Something about his nature was such that he was incapable of playing it cool or blending in. He certainly didn't have the ability that I did.

I figured that's why the headaches were coming regularly, like there was another person inside trying to get out. If I was successful, the headaches would stop but there might be hell to pay nevertheless.

I gave the doc some answer I thought he would absorb like a sponge and forget about. Something to the effect of having become someone far more responsible than he ever considered, and being afraid at times by that responsibility. He nodded slowly, seeming to agree with me, accept the so-called dilemma I felt. His eyes narrowed as though he was trying to get small enough to get inside me. This old man, wrinkled, white hair, fluffy eyebrows, bags under his eyes, was a lot smarter than those college professors in Wichita. He didn't need the benefit of any scientific tests to determine an issue with a patient. I was sure he was the only one who could help me but, at the same time, the one I should not trust too much.

He gave me some spiel about Freud and

psychoanalysis. Every time he read a new book about something medical, he was eager to use it as a reference, as though those books were written to help him explain me out to myself. I listened as I always did, patiently and with respect. I was never going to tell him that the answers weren't found in a book.

It might have been a mistake to go back to him so soon after my physical. If I had just had some hooch and a few aspirin, it would have made it more tolerable and then I wouldn't have had to open this can of worms. He reminded me of my dad—at least the kindness part and not so much the education. Dr. Brenz really cared, which made my regular visits all the more painful.

My thoughts turned back to the guy in the hotel. I had a feeling deep in my gut he would be one to stir up things far worse than the doc could. Dr. Brenz might be capable of disrupting my life but it felt like this guy was a hound dog just itching to chase rabbits. If that hound ever got rabid, it'd have to be put down hard. It seemed like the hunt was on.

Chapter Twelve

Jake convinced Heather to go with him to the Fifth Avenue Theater. He could see she was getting more and more bored, going stir crazy just sitting around, and itching to get out now the warmth of the summer was here. A year had passed and she had gone shopping a few times, went out to dinner with Jake once or twice, and did her best with the *Traveler*'s crossword puzzle. Jake was too busy playing the part of a working class stiff, just another Joe in a factory making a cheap dollar and waiting on a dream. The problem was it was no play acting; he was doing it rather than sliding by, with a steak dinner and all the trimmings.

Ironically, the show that was playing was *Manhattan Melodrama*. Jake didn't tell her it was the last movie John Dillinger watched before the Feds plugged him. He was smiling throughout the show. He couldn't remember the last time he had a reason to smile.

Just outside the theater, Jake saw Phil Garmes standing by himself and starting to light a cigarette. Jake walked over briskly and scratched a match with his thumb. Phil instinctively leaned into it, lit his smoke, and then looked up at the grinning man.

"You know who I am?" Jake asked in a hoarse whisper.

"Yeah. The guy from 2B."

"You don't recognize me?"

Phil nodded negatively. He wasn't sure what the answer should have been.

"Jake Hickey? 'Crazy' Jake?"

"I'm sorry, sir…"

The breath was starting to get harder to hold on to, and Phil was set to take a step back when Jake interrupted. "You ever hear of 'Bugs' Moran?"

Phil grew a smile, happy to have at least one correct answer available. "Yes, sir. One of them Chicago guys…"

"Well, I'm his partner."

The smile shrank faster than Phil's member after a quick encounter with a hoochie coochie gal. Anyone with half a brain knew such men existed not only in the newspaper but, more likely than not, right there in Arkansas City. Nothing like this wild-eyed man had ever crossed his path. Jake knew what kind of sleaze this kid was, seeing him salivate like a juicy T-bone was on the plate in front of him. Jake figured Phil would not let a good opportunity get away.

"Yes, sir." It was the right response: respectful while not allowing a note of doubt to enter. The kind of tone a lackey would make when talking to a boss.

"Who runs the action in this town?" Jake spoke quickly. He had questions and needed fast answers. Phil's eyes grew wide, like hard boiled eggs. There was a slight shaking of his head like he had just entered a barn with a wild stallion in heat and the door was closing behind him. "Come on, kid. You've gotten me some hooch. You placed a few bets for me. There's more going on in this town than that. Right?"

Jake's eyes got wide as well but with a sort of

manic excitement. This was the tip of the iceberg. From what George had mentioned in the past, there could have been several guys like him in the area, all cooling off for a spell, all itching to get their fingers wrapped back around a trigger.

"I…don't…know…" It was like Death staring Phil in the face. All the articles about Pretty Boy Flood hiding out somewhere in the area, maybe just down over the border in Oklahoma, maybe in someone's house down the street, seemed like a fable or a spook story. No one could imagine it right here and right in front of them. Phil Garmes was a slick guy who could do a few favors off the cuff for the more well off guests and make an extra quarter here or dollar there. There was a certain sense of importance, being The Man, and now realizing he was small potatoes in the big picture.

"Look, you find out who runs things here. You don't have to set up any intros or even approach anybody. You find out and there'll be some serious jack in your pocket. You understand?"

This was the big opportunity Phil Garmes had always been waiting for, and now he was about to melt away. It was as though Myrna Loy herself had asked him to dance and all he could do was wet his pants. Not willing to let this one go, he braced himself with the last morsel of courage he had, stood up straight, and looked at Jake clearly in the eyes.

"I'll let you know what I find, sir."

Jake gave him a friendly pat on the shoulder and stuck a dollar bill in his shirt pocket.

It was two days later when Giuseppe Gallo called Jake into the big office. Martin Childers sat in a large wide winged back leather chair smoking a tightly wrapped cigar. He didn't flinch when Hickey entered the room. Jake took a seat in a wooden chair just to the side where he was only able to look at Childers' profile, the smoke coming from him giving him the appearance of a mad bull.

"Mr. Gallo here says you've been an exemplary employee."

Jake was at a crossroads. He had been hanging out in this town for a while, working tirelessly, putting away a few dollars, and hearing nothing from his old Chicago mates. While it might be true that patience was a virtue, he had no desire to continue being virtuous. He might just as easily have gotten killed in the Windy City, not biding his time, acting irrationally, too eager for Moran to push to take over the rackets, probably winding up upsetting the Mob. At this moment, he could play nice and wind up being a cheesy underling or press the matter and push for entry into whatever scam was going on here and now.

"Who are you, mister?" Jake went full speed ahead.

"Name's Childers. I operate the Kanotex Refinery."

"And Mr. Gallo says I'm a good worker."

"Yes. I'd like you to come work for me." Childers turned in his chair, looking directly at Jake, and continuing to let a fine stream of smoke blow in his direction.

"Why would I want to do that, Mr. Childers?"

"Let's say there'd be more opportunities for professional advancement. In these difficult times, a smart man with talent can go a long way." Childers turned back, sitting straight up, chin pointing out, a scowl forming on his brow. "Unless you'd rather stay with the rabble who have not the slightest hope in the world."

Either Phil Garmes had made the correct inquiries or someone had him pegged from the moment he got into town. This is what Jake wanted all along but he didn't appreciate how it was coming out. He thought George was sending him to a boring field of sunflowers. Turns out it was the lion's den and he was being played the whole time. If they knew who he was, why didn't they approach him sooner? How was it that he couldn't spot one of them and figure out their play? It finally occurred to him his *Crazy* Jake reputation had preceded him, and they wanted to make sure he was cool headed and ready to do some work. Serious work.

Jake leaned back in his chair, wrapping his hands on the back of his head. It was time to see where this Childers stood.

"Sounds intriguing, Mr. Childers. I'd like to talk about the pay and other benefits."

Martin Childers shot up faster than a roman candle and stood directly over Jake. The cigar was clenched in his teeth with spittle dribbling onto his chin. He pulled it sharply and practically spit as he spoke. "Listen to me, you Mick punk. This is a one-time offer. I walk out that door and you're left slaving your miserable life away in a packing plant. You act tough with the people I tell you to act tough with. But not with me. Do you understand?"

Now the cards were on the table. All the players were identified. Childers probably thought an attitude like that could scare Jake. All it had done was shown him his hand. He could be polite and respectable now, knowing Childers had a weak spot he could exploit.

"I know how it works, Mr. Childers."

He stood up, taking his place alongside Childers, and nodded toward the office door, letting his new boss lead the way.

Chapter Thirteen

I couldn't fight off Beth Handy's charms any longer. I escorted her one evening to Albert's Drugs and bought her a sundae complete with chocolate syrup and whipped cream and nuts and a cherry while I sipped a vanilla cola. We sat in a booth, me looking away most of the time, certainly not wanting to become entrapped by her soft innocent eyes as well as being self-conscious at how I looked. When it came to Big Ray or George McAllister, or any of the guys, it didn't really matter. With the possibility of encountering a murder victim, you figured they were supposed to be prepared to look at something ungodly. Somehow I just felt incomplete around Beth, like I wasn't all that I should be. It might have been I didn't know her as well as I thought I should.

To her credit, she ate slowly like a lady, looking up after each bite and trying to gaze into my eyes. She would never have acted strange around me. To her, I was still the teenage Baron Witherspoon, the young and good-looking guy who had his whole life ahead of him. I had this vague recollection somewhere in the past of being more comfortable around girls in general, even wanting them. Now, I felt I couldn't make any connection beyond common courtesy. I could look at Beth, admire her gentility, but feel as though I was looking at her from afar, at times with no real sense of where I was.

"I've probably asked you before," she said, "but does it hurt much?"

"What?"

"The scars."

"Not any more. Used to, but that was long ago. Besides, it wasn't really the scars that hurt."

"Oh. What was it then?"

"The memories." I had said it and it was the truth. Perhaps she didn't understand. Maybe she couldn't understand. She was destined to be that hometown girl who would never experience any of the excitement of the great big world out there. Then again, she would never have to go through any of its pain either. This town was all she would ever need.

She took a few more bites of her sundae trying to fill these quiet moments with something important to say. "So why is it you never became a poet like your Mom wanted you to?"

"A poet in Ark City? I never knew of one."

She let her spoon clink in her class, mockingly dismayed at my lack of knowledge. "Roy Farrell Greene."

"Who?"

"Roy Farrell Greene. He wrote a book of poems called *Cupid is King.*"

"Oh. And where is he now?"

Her eyes looked down as though her lead in some imagined race had just vanished. "He's dead. He died a while back."

"Guess there's no future in being a poet." The smirk that pretended to be a smile let her know I wasn't all serious.

I kept looking around, noticing details of things I had seen so many times and feeling disconnected, like this was the first time I had been in Albert's Drugs and this was my first vanilla cola, instead of being something I had done countless times. There were too many periods recently where I felt out of place despite the pride I had doing my job. It was as though I was placed here in this city at this moment in time to perform some task or do something extraordinary. I could never figure out what it was supposed to be. I was never all that religious growing up yet I sensed it was like something out of the Old Testament, kind of like an angel who had been sent on a mission to be here. It felt silly thinking that. I knew for a fact I was no angel. All the while, I continued to wish I could just be like one of them.

"If you want to know the truth, Baron," Beth continued in a haughty tone, "my father's been wanting me to see Frank Appleby, maybe even marry him. Do you have any thoughts on that?"

It was just like Ms. Elizabeth Handy to pop out with some question in the hopes of throwing me off my guard somehow, forgetting I had seen enough shocking things to last a lifetime. I could only wind up smiling; it was my way of undercutting her efforts, and at the same time make her realize I was onto her game.

"Sounds like a splendid idea, Ms. Handy. Mr. Appleby is a fine upstanding gentleman who has a great deal of prospects worthy of a lady like yourself."

She smiled back. There was nothing else she could do. She knew deep down I could never commit to her, not because of my facial scarring but because I didn't have a future, much less a past. I had no desire to be a detective or work my way up in the department. Being a patrol cop was all I was going to do. Ever. I figured after the doctors in France saved my life and gave me enough of a face to be moderately acceptable, I was given a second chance, another life. But this one wasn't turning out so well. I knew people liked me and respected what I did. By the same token, no one had ever been able to get close enough to me to know who I really was. Perhaps much of that was my fault but I never really complained. It's a strange feeling trying to fit in, wanting to fit in, but knowing you don't belong. You can call someone by their name but that doesn't define them. Nearly sixteen years and I still had nothing more than a name.

"It's kind of nice having some bigwigs in town."

"How do you mean?" I asked, not being aware of anyone really important having visited recently.

"The lady living in the Gladstone. She bought a couple of real nice hats from my dad this week. Real expensive, like the kind ladies from Kansas City buy. My dad said she'd been in once or twice before, asked questions like she knew what she was talking about, but didn't buy anything."

It seemed like she was referring to the lady who was with the man in the fancy car. That hatbox she delivered to Phil was obviously for them. By Beth saying the lady was living in the hotel, it made me wonder even more who the guy was. I recall Phil Garmes trying to sell me a tale about this fella being on hard times having lost his dough up north. If that were the case, it didn't seem like he was the type to be affording fancy hats. It could only mean he was more than Phil thought he was, unless Phil knew more than he was saying. It would be easy to squeeze it from him considering he had a low tolerance for the very thought of pain. However, I wasn't looking to let anyone get excited on this. If it turned out to be nothing and I made it look like something, I'd have one angry man on my hands. On the other side of the coin was something I had felt all along: this city had a hornet's nest hidden somewhere and you didn't get them angry else you'd get stung.

"Bet your father was plum happy about that." I tried my best to sound like I was letting it slide.

"That ain't the best part."

"Oh yeah?"

"Lady said she'd be back for more, that things were looking up for her."

After I saw Beth back to her home, I took a stroll by the Gladstone. I was in a plain white shirt and pants, not in my uniform. Phil Garmes, standing out front smoking a cigarette, didn't notice me until I was right up on him.

"Hey, Baron. I guess it's okay to call you that when you're not in uniform, huh?"

"Had my way, I'd prefer you not call me anything." It was important not to be too nice to him then he would think something was up.

Phil's smile cut wide from ear to ear, toothy like a set of shears, eyes sparkling with a glow of satisfaction. It wasn't his usual self but a bigger and more obnoxious version as though he were sitting on top of the world and everyone was bowing at his feet.

"That's fine by me. I'm in too good of a mood to really care all that much."

"Why's that?"

"There's others who appreciate my efforts."

It made no sense to push the inquiry. It was obvious he had done something to get into someone's good graces. Knowing Phil, I could see him pushing the issue and making himself seem more important than he really was, somewhat like that blabbermouth Will Bell. That kind of attitude don't settle too well with the people holding the big stick. I really couldn't abide people like Phil but, all the same, I almost felt like telling him to be careful. Naturally, he wouldn't have taken my advice so it was best not even giving it.

From what I could gather, there was more activity going on in the past few months than there had been in several years. It all seemed to start with the arrival of that guy in the fancy car and his doll. If I was right, the powder kegs were being piled up and all it would take is one spark to blow it sky high. It was time for me to take more notice and start looking into the dark corners.

Chapter Fourteen

Chief Taylor called me into his office one morning when he saw me coming in for the start of my shift. His matter-of-fact attitude covered an urgency I knew too well. When I stepped in, he instructed me to close the door and sit on the chair in front of his desk. Most of my younger co-workers might have taken that as preceding an act of discipline. I knew when Chief Taylor was ready for a reprimand; his eyes blazed red as the devil.

"Read these and tell me what you make of them." He handed me a series of teletype printouts. They all described bank robberies. Wellington. Winfield. Caldwell. Sedan. In Oklahoma, there was Ponca City, Blackwell, Enid, and Perry. All of these took place within the last couple of weeks. Two- or three-man teams. All wearing black suits and black hats with scarves around their faces. Quick entry, fast moving, harsh and fearful language, in and out in less than three minutes. If I didn't know better, I'd have sworn Dillinger himself had moved down here. Of course, Dillinger was dead and there wasn't anyone as good at this as him, at least that I knew of for sure.

"Notice anything?" Whereas it was frustrating to feel like a schoolboy taking his final exam, I appreciated the fact the chief trusted my experience enough to get my feedback. In my mind, I had a map of the area and started placing dots on it where the robberies took place. It seemed like it was all in a bubble around our town, Arkansas City. None of it was close enough to be noticeable. All of them were positioned enough to make this their center.

"What do you think, Chief?"

"Nothing yet. I just saw these from the pile and figured the same thing you just came up with. No sense in reading too much into it. It might be just a coincidence."

I must have had that squinty look on my face, the one I get when I start thinking too hard, because the chief raised an eyebrow and peered at me like I was a suspect he was interrogating. I laid out my concerns from the past several months, my recent encounter with Phil Garmes, the fancy dandy and his dame and the car at the Gladstone, and how this guy seemed to be working at the packing plant. He fairly identified where these could all be quite innocent aspects, then also said they could add up to something. It wasn't a good idea to press this guy without knowing what we were pressing him for. On the other hand, keeping an eye on him might lead to uncovering illegal activity.

"You need someone on this with you?" As much as that comment and the trust it implied made me feel like a true detective, I knew this was going to have to be something I did on my own. The younger guys would not have been able to keep their big mouth shut and the older guys wouldn't have been able to keep up with me. For the most part, with my facial scars, the people who didn't know me often just stayed away, not knowing how to respond to me. That would make it easier for me to watch them.

"Be easy enough to do on my own."

He nodded, lightly at first in agreement, and then heavier as though there was a great weight upon him. "I don't like this, Baron." His voice was thick with emotion, as though the reports of these robberies were like a death in his family. "You remember Uncle Billy?"

He was referring to William Gray, a former U.S. deputy marshal, constable, deputy sheriff, and police officer here in town. He was never shot during his long and distinguished career and never had to shoot a man to arrest him.

"I was at his funeral last year. A lot of us were." I didn't know him personally but his stories were the stuff of legend.

"Uncle Billy got it done without it getting ugly. I've got a bad feeling this is going to get ugly."

I could only nod back in agreement. I wouldn't validate his concerns by showing fear. I had learned a long time ago that showing fear doesn't get you out of a bad situation any more than acting brave. You just had to do what was necessary when the time came.

For the next several days, I made sure my beat took me somewhere in the vicinity of the Gladstone. I knew Phil Garmes was aware of this but it didn't really matter. When it came right down to it, he was just like a possum that would freeze up at the first sign of trouble. I didn't see the car outside the packing plant and began to wonder if maybe the guy had skipped town. I soon learned otherwise when I was roaming around Junior's.

Junior's was a juke joint, a private club with paid membership for local good old boys. Even though I didn't pay, I had a standing membership on account of my service in the Great War. There were a few gentlemen who had been down in Cuba for the Spanish-American War and they told some tall tales. You would have sworn each and every one of them had ridden with Colonel Roosevelt.

The place had music and food and a piano player slapping the keys with the latest style of music. They were also rumored to have a back room with gambling and drinks. My membership didn't take me that far. But they knew I didn't care much to hassle them, which is another reason why I was allowed to come in. Everyone there was a long-time resident of the city. Except for the dandy and his girl. He was shaking everyone's hand, a blowhard who had known them for ages, talking loud and blustery with enough wind to blow the sails of a prairie wagon. The woman was dolled up all set to meet the Queen of England. Our eyes met and she made me feel like the King. Without a word, she stood up like a cat does when it's all done sleeping, and sauntered over to me.

"Howdy, Sherriff."

I smiled, knowing it was pointless to try to explain my status with the police force. She would just think I was a quaint hick, not knowing the truth. She pulled out a cigarette from a fancy engraved case and placed it between her lips like it was a delicate thing, and then looked at me with an eyebrow raised as though she was a lapper. I flicked my nail against a match in my pocket without taking my eyes off her. There was a glistening in her eyes as the flame burned in front of her. She smiled, blowing the first smoke out and up over my shoulder.

Her fella sauntered over as well, only it was more

like a freight train roaring down a track. It was then I noticed he was wearing spats, which I hadn't seen anyone wear since I was taking care of some business with a lawyer in Wichita over ten years ago. That style of fancy dress just didn't seem to fit in around here. Neither did he.

"Don't believe we've met." He stuck his hand out directly at my gut. "Jack Hale."

"Baron Witherspoon," I responded. I turned toward the lady and added, "Officer Baron Witherspoon." She smiled and realized I was no rube. "What brings you to Ark City, Mr. Hale?"

"Ark City? Oh, yeah. That's what you guys call it. Funny thing, huh? Well, you know, times being hard and all, I figured I'd get me a fresh start."

"If you don't mind my saying so, a fella like you with a lot of class and all, well, this doesn't seem like the place you'd want to go for a fresh start."

"Well, that's where you're wrong, Officer." He poked my shoulder with the hand holding his cigarette, just like an energetic guy from a big city would do, then realized it seemed a little inappropriate. He brought his hand up and took a drag of the cigarette all in one complete move, kind of like he was used to getting himself out of trouble. "There's more unemployment in the big cities than there is in the farmland and rural areas. Business is hurting but farmers and factories are still thriving for hard working men like me. Sure, there are differences, what you might call a certain lack of conveniences," he continued, looking quickly at the lady. He then stood close to her, putting his arm around her waist. "But we'll get by just fine." He had the same wide smile I'd seen on Phil Garmes, almost as though they were kin.

"What city did you come from?" I asked as nonchalant as I could. His face changed from big and broad and outgoing to all scrunched up as though he didn't want to let me guide the discussion.

"Chicago." It seemed like it was painful for him to say it.

"Oh, really. Where about?"

"A neighborhood you probably never heard of." That smile was coming out, like the sun peeking through the clouds after a storm.

"Try me." I smiled, all friendly like, but closer to being a cat cornering a rat.

Mr. Hale's swagger returned, figuring he could say what he wanted with the notion that I hadn't been more than fifty miles in any direction of this city.

"Called Lincoln Park."

"North Side, right?"

"You've heard of it?"

"I've heard of it." My face went blank, stiff, cold. I was surprised neither the doll nor the guy made any comment about my scars, didn't ask any questions, just accepted me like it was a normal thing. He never looked away from me, didn't let the sight of my scars dissuade him. This told me he was either polite or had seen far worse.

He gave me his big confident smile, and nodded. He couldn't tell if I was a book smart farmer boy or something else.

"Well, what do you know? I figure we best be going. Got the job to go to tomorrow. You know how it is?" He guided her by the waist out and toward the door as though there were a fire in the building. It seemed like she was swaying with a little extra sass in the caboose, as though she were waving goodbye to me in some cryptic way.

Lincoln Park was the neighborhood where the SMC Cartage warehouse was located. It was where seven members of Bugs Moran's gang were lined up against a wall and executed by men many claimed were sent by Al Capone. This was the famous St. Valentine's Day Massacre. It could have been a coincidence this tough pug was just another Irish kid from the neighborhood. Or maybe he was somebody who knew somebody. I couldn't tell despite a sting in the back of my neck.

I had heard of Lincoln Park but not the way he thought I did.

He was older, perhaps around my age, and looked like a grownup version of someone I thought I remembered. It was tough to tell. Dr. Brenz would probably have referred to these memory lapses as "war trauma" or some other expression he'd read from one of his books. I didn't want to make any assumptions about the guy but I was glad to finally meet up face to face with him.

She, on the other hand, was no one I had ever seen before, and I don't mean from memory. Not even in Europe during the War had I encountered a gal put together so intently. If she were a garage mechanic, she would have had all the tools to fix my engine. Somehow I got the notion that was her intention.

Chapter Fifteen

Heather Devore was light on her feet and acting giggly, and it wasn't from the cheap hooch at Junior's. She had been in this dusty and dull little town, this Arkansas City (which could have been the state of Arkansas itself for all she knew or cared), watching time pass slowly, feeling the life being drained from her, mere months seeming like years. There were no silk sheets or jazz bands or other girls to pal around with. The only tough talking guy was Jake and hearing him all by himself seemed like a broken phonograph. She was used to the nightlife but this burg rolled up its sidewalks by sundown.

Junior's was no Halligan's or Marge's Still and the piano player sure as hell wasn't Fats Waller. At the very least, there was booze and music and a lot of men noticing her in her fine duds and new hat. This took the edge off living here for the unforeseeable future. She figured she might be extra special nice to Jake that night.

It seemed like he had loosened up a bit, holding her tight around the waist and walking like they owned the town. He had his woman on his hip and nothing could stand in his way. Who knows? Maybe with the way things were going, this dump could turn out to be Little Chicago after all. There was a feeling of comfort and warmth being so close and snug to him. He felt so relaxed he had a smile on his face rather than that worn and tight frown. For this one evening, everything was just fine, just the way it should be.

Jake didn't make a comment to Phil Garmes as he passed through the lobby, didn't so much as grunt or nod. Heather was tight lipped but nodded lightly with encouragement. Right then, she was the focus of Jake's attention and not all the business that was going on. He opened the door to the room for her. Before she had a chance to turn on the light, Jake's arm flew in a big roundhouse, smacking her face hard with a loud slap, an instant sting and burn emanating from her cheek down her chin and up to her eyes which started watering. His emerald signet ring caught her cheekbone, which started throbbing. He turned on the light, staring directly at her, freezing her with his gaze.

"What the hell do you think you were doing?" He spoke sharply through a clenched jaw and lips tighter than a stretched inner tube. Spit flew from his mouth with each word. His eyes had turned black, and all the color had drained from his face. "You acted like some gold-digger togged to the bricks having a ring-a-ding-ding. It's one thing for these rubes to be looking at you like your next week's meal. But what was that thing with the copper? You know I've been sweating it out there trying to put together a bankroll for us and you're getting all cozy with Johnny Law."

Heather was shaking, tears rolling down her eyes, face now numb except for where the ring struck her like a cattle brand. In a brief moment, there was the exhilarating feeling of hope that faded into the realization she was trapped in a box no bigger than a casket. She was caught in a tin shed with a tornado spinning around and nowhere to go. There was a vision of her own death, but it wasn't cold and dark. It was in a hotel in Arkansas City, Kansas with the lights on, lying on a bed with four empty walls.

Jake grabbed her roughly by the shoulders and completely decimated her dress, leaving her standing there stark naked. A violent chill ran through her, hardening her nipples to the point of bursting. She was not the seductive dolly she thought she was. Just another dumb Dora who was only able to live off her looks and her body. What Jake had in mind at that moment was going to go a long way toward taking away both.

In the morning, *Crazy* Jake had returned to being the sassy little dandy he presented to everyone else. She heard him humming a tune they heard last night while he was shaving. She contemplated that straight razor, the image of shaving his stubble, and wondering if she would ever have the gumption to use it for something more permanent. She was good and had been for a long time. She couldn't help wonder if he was looking for something better, even right here in this little town. Something fresh and clean and looking for a hoot and a holler he could teach new things. It would take everything to have to keep him interested while considering how to leave him at the same time.

Heather lay in bed, naked under the sheet, the coppery taste of blood in her mouth, feeling the throb and heat of bruises on her body without actually looking for them. It wouldn't be necessary. Jake's brutality was something she had never experienced directly. She had seen what he could do to underlings, watched him beat a guy in front of George Moran to prove his worth. There were rough drunken bouts of sex in a couple of Chicago hotels but none of it was about demoralizing her, putting her down, or wiping her out. This time was different. She knew no one here, didn't have friends to turn to or even other gangsters who would take her under their wing. Her life now was completely dependent upon Jake Hickey.

He came out from the bathroom, spruced up like a dapper dandy. He looked at her as he always did with a kind of casualness that didn't actually reveal anything. Maybe that was his way of saying "No hard feelings. Everything is okay. We're going to be fine." It left her feeling uncomfortable not knowing what was to happen next.

"Make sure you get dolled up tonight. We're going out."

"Where to, Jake?" Her voice had the pretended sound of eagerness. It came from the deepest pits of desperation.

"Never you mind. But there's some people I need to impress. Don't disappoint me."

He left abruptly. She slowly got out of bed, working through the pain in her arms and back and butt and groin. A long hot bath would help her recover. It would also give her time to think of a plan, something that might involve the officer she met last night.

Chapter Sixteen

Big Ray was laid low with the flu—at least that's what he said. My guess was a hangover. He had good intentions but poor execution. The Chief wanted extra patrols on Friday night since it was payday, and we had been getting more than our share of drunk and disorderly violations. The desk sergeant asked me to pull some overtime to help out. I was never like some of the veterans, complaining they put in their time on night patrols and didn't have to do that sort of stuff any more. The fact I still did made some of them have a beef with me. Nobody said anything, but this was one reason I got along with the younger guys better. I recognized something in them I had once, something the old-timers could no longer see, or just plain forgot about.

On nights like these, we all had a route, more or less circular, that crossed over each other. Every so often, we would pass another patrolman. Depending on where your route was, you might pass three or four other guys. It was designed for safety, the fact we were never more than fifteen minutes away from each other. We would stop at the intersection and get caught up on what might be going on. George McAllister always wanted to talk too much and usually not about anything relating to work.

"You know, that Davis girl's been making eyes at

me. Every time I go into the mercantile."

"Is that a fact?" I was willing to give George a little rope. After that, I'd trip him up.

"That is a fact."

"Maybe she's wondering what you're doing coming in four, five times a week and not buying anything."

"Now, wait a minute, Baron…"

"Keep your eyes open, George. It's a little too quiet tonight."

When I talked serious, he knew it was time to let the stories pass. His look of efficiency was all I needed to know that he was ready for it, whatever might happen. I had known George the longest of all the guys. He was always ready to be a cop but not always happy about it. The story went he had a boyhood friend who had become a wildcatter down in Texas, struck big with the company he was working for, then wound up opening his own hardware store down around San Antonio. The guy had a wife and a kid and a house. George often brought him up in conversation. What he failed to mention was all the years his friend broke his back and going hungry before he hit big. George always felt it was going to be easier than it actually was.

It was past midnight when I passed Dave Morton. He was one of the new guys just down from outside of Andover. He wasn't much of a farmer. Then again, Kansas was not a kind place to most farmers in the 20's. Nevertheless, his father told him to enlist in the Marines or get a job as a policeman. He seemed to be doing fine although he acted as straight as a Marine. I'm sure he wanted to loosen up and be a pal only he wasn't sure how. We were down near the end of

Chestnut Street, approaching the railroad tracks.

"I swear, I thought I saw a shadow of something." Dave kept looking over my shoulder, eyes wide as a cat.

"A person?"

"Not sure."

"I'll check it on my pass."

"Want me to go with you?"

"No. That's why we do these routes. I'll blow my whistle if I come across anything." Dave kept looking back at me as I moved on toward the direction from which he had just come. It wasn't long before I eventually saw what he had seen: a figure in the shadows along a fence near the railroad tracks. I thought at first it might be Rogelio Lopez, reckoning he would be the one I was most likely to encounter. The figure was taller and broader and, as he moved out of the shadows, blonder. Like Rogelio, he had a bottle in one hand but what appeared to be an automatic in the other. I wasn't all that concerned thinking he might have been just another mill worker overdoing it with his paycheck. But when our eyes finally met, I saw the rage of a whirlwind and the unrelenting power of a twister. This was not a man to be trifled with considering the passion spewing forth from his pores.

"What are you doing here, boy?" he yelled, spit flying from his mouth.

"Been drinking a bit, friend?"

"I ain't your friend, sonny."

Blowing my whistle would have aroused him further. Talking to him was my only chance except I wasn't too sure what to say. He wasn't anyone I recognized, and certainly not from around these parts originally. "Nobody wants any trouble."

"Oh, but that's all you're gonna get. And plenty of it." He took a slug from the bottle never once taking his eyes off me, and holding the gun down by his side, ever at the ready.

"Well, you're calling the shots."

"You're damn right." He yelled straight at me, like I was his son and had done something extremely wrong. "We're calling the shots. We're running things here. You're just a janitor cleaning up the mess."

Even in his drunken state, he still had the confidence and wherewithal to take violent action. Since I was the only one in the area, it would most definitely be directed at me. The best I could hope for was to get him yelling more and louder, hoping one of the other guys would hear it.

"So, who'd you say was running things? I don't think I caught that."

"Why're you askin'?"

His words were slurring but he was getting louder.

"Well, so's I don't run afoul of you boys. I ain't so sure I want to make anyone upset. You know what I mean?"

And then, it all happened too quickly:

He took another swig, long and drawn out.

I took one half-step forward.

His gun hand moved, didn't come up exactly, but moved more than it had.

I withdrew my piece and fired at the shoulder opposite his gun hand.

He fired his gun almost instinctively but it went into the ground.

He raised his gun.

I fired again, hitting just above his left knee.

He didn't fall. Instead he kept firing wildly and screaming.

I aimed for his chest and wound up shooting him in the throat.

By the time George and Dave arrived the blond was facedown on the ground, lying in his own blood, which was draining faster than dirty water out of a bathtub. It smelled like a battlefield, smoke choking my lungs, for a moment bringing me back to the forest and the war.

It was sixteen years since I killed a man. Back then it was the enemy. I don't know who it was this time.

A profound exhaustion dropped over me as a truck drove up to bring the body to Dr. Brenz's office.

The next morning, I took a hot bath and was surprised to find Mrs. McGuire had some homemade biscuits and jam and real hot black coffee for me, long after she would have had breakfast available for any other tenant. It made the morning feel more normal, although I knew it wouldn't last that way for long.

Because of that full belly and hot coffee, I surprised Chief Taylor with my energy and enthusiasm. It wasn't that I was happy with the outcome from last night. All things being equal, it was better him than me. I sat comfortably opposite the chief.

"The doc confirm the findings?" I knew I was not going to be held responsible and that the shooting was justified. But you always wanted to hear it official.

"Didn't have to. Councilman Hallett cleared you."

My face went numb like it used to years ago after the surgeries. This time it was something I could never have expected. "What's he got to do with anything? He wasn't even there."

The chief leaned forward over his desk, holding a file with a single sheet of paper. "Hallett got over to Dr. Brenz's office after you went home. They conferred and decided this was self-defense and no charges would be pressed. Then he had the body taken away."

"Who did?"

"Hallett."

"Why?"

"Didn't say."

I stood up, charged by the coffee and my growing anger. We didn't have a lot of shootings in Ark City but there was a protocol to follow. Politicians didn't conduct medical exams or determine causes of death. They sure didn't decide what to do with a corpse in a police investigation.

"What do you mean he didn't say? Who was the guy I shot? What was he doing out there?"

"The councilman said he talked to Martin Childers. It was one of his guys out on a bender."

"I've never seen the guy before."

"Said he was new in town."

"I'm not buying it."

"Gonna have to, Baron. The councilman says the case is closed, then it's closed."

"When were you ever one to back down like this?"

There must have been too much moxie in the tone of my voice because Chief Taylor rose like a buzzard over a dead rabbit and looked like he was ready to chew me to pieces. He closed and locked his door, standing before it. I felt him behind me but at this point was too afraid to turn around.

"What was it you were mentioning to George

McAlister last night? Something about what the guy said?"

My shoulders eased, and my back was no longer stiff. My resistance was about gone, so I turned slightly in my chair, looking at him over my shoulder. "Said *We* were calling the shots and *We* were running things."

"He didn't say who they were?"

"No, sir."

I knew he was going to tell me to back off this one, even forget about following the guy from the Gladstone. I had this bad feeling Chief Taylor was taking money like many others and this time was going to look away rather than let me loose. He surprised me by leaning down and speaking quietly into my ear, not quite a whisper but something just as confidential. "Something bad is going on, Officer Witherspoon. Something really bad if Hallett makes a personal call. You need to push ahead." He walked around his desk, sitting in his big seat, leaning back straight and firm. "But you need to be careful. I don't know who you can trust."

It was gratifying to receive that level of confidence. Then again, I didn't know who would be there for me if I got in over my head. The chief may have been clean, or he might have respected me more than the money coming his way. I really didn't know. All I knew was that as soon as I left his office I was walking the road alone.

Chapter Seventeen

The fact that Councilman Hallett was involved meant the graft ran high as well as deep. At this point, anyone could be involved. Whereas I doubted Chief Taylor knew what was going on, he acted as though he couldn't make a call on this, perhaps out of fear of repercussion, for what I couldn't be sure. I had never known him to be like that before. I was guessing maybe there were things I didn't know about him, same as there were things he had no idea about me.

I went back to the shooting scene and walked around near the fence. I kicked the ground hoping it would reveal the answers. I wound up finding nine .32 ACP shells. I was trying to remember what the gun looked like but all I could see in my mind were those big eyes as though the man was possessed. I had never encountered him around at all before, not at the refinery or the mercantile or the diner. He was certainly not as conspicuous as the guy with the fancy car at Junior's that night. It would be difficult figuring out who he was when you considered this whole thing was made to vanish like a magician's trick.

Dave Morton sauntered over, hands in pocket, looking like he had run out of ideas. "Shells?" he asked, looking at my hand.

"Yep. Nine of 'em."

"That makes sense. I'm almost sure it was a

Savage Model 1907."

"You saw it?"

"Yeah. When I came running back to find you."

"Great. Maybe we can get prints off it and try to figure out..."

Dave shook his head. The race seemed over before it started. "I'm sorry, Baron. I didn't mean we had the gun. As a matter of fact, that's why I was coming back here. I saw it on the ground right after the shooting. I took a quick glance at it when I was checking out to see if the guy was dead or not. Then I ran over to you. I haven't seen it since."

"Maybe it's back at the station house."

Dave kept shaking his head. It was getting frustrating and annoying.

"I checked there already," he said. "I don't know where it could be. There were only a bunch of other cops around. Maybe one of them has it."

His innocent little comment made more sense than he realized.

It felt awkward going to Kanotex in my street clothes to see Martin Childers. If I were wearing my uniform, it would have appeared more professional. Then again, if half the cops in the city were in his pocket as the rumors implied, the notion of *official* didn't mean all that much. His secretary didn't seem to pay me much heed until I indicated I was with the police. After that, she was just dubious.

"A Baron Witherspoon is here to see you," she said blandly, sticking her wet red lips into the Flexifone.

"Officer Witherspoon," I corrected but she made no effort to follow suit.

Martin Childers emerged from behind a big oak

door buttoning his jacket as though whatever went on prior was not as important as this meeting he was about to have with me. His hand warmly extended, he expressed deep concerned. "Baron, I'm pleased to see you're well. I take it you weren't shot."

His handshake could have substituted for any of the machinery in the plant.

"No, sir. Fortunately not."

He put his arm around my shoulder, guiding us toward his private office while at the same time looking back over his shoulder to advise his secretary to hold all calls. Once inside, the office appeared to be almost as big as my entire apartment. He motioned toward a large wing-backed chair in front of a mammoth oak desk, devoid of anything except the intercom speaker, a phone, a green-globed lamb, and a blotter. Behind the desk was a small sideboard with crystal glasses, an ice bucket, and several decanters with various shades of brown liquids. He started to reach for a glass, then turned and after placing the stopper back in the decanter.

"I was about to offer you a whisky. But then I realized that, even with the repeal of prohibition, Kansas is still a dry state and you're a police officer." The recognition of his own *crime* was more of a challenge than anything. It was a game men like him enjoyed playing. Such a show of power and lack of respect for the law waited for a response. If there was none, they won the game. I passed on over it, not in the mood to get my foot caught in the bear trap.

"I'm told the man who was killed last night worked here."

He took his time lighting his cigar, drawing deep

and blowing out the smoke in a straight path toward the ceiling. You could marvel at how bullet straight the smoke projected. "I don't know where you got that information."

"Councilman Hallett. He told Chief Taylor."

"I'm terribly sorry you have been misled, Baron. But everyone who works here has been accounted for."

"You have any idea why the councilman would say such a thing?"

"I haven't the slightest notion." The smile let me know he knew I had nothing. This was like René Lacoste and Bill Tilden, artfully swatting the ball back and forth over the net. It could go on forever to no avail.

"Sorry to bother you." I stood to leave. I'd have to find answers somewhere else.

Childers came from behind his desk, right hand down by his side with the smoldering cigar, left hand around my shoulder in a fatherly and comforting fashion. "From what I heard, it was all a terrible incident. A man too drunk to know better. You did your job well, Officer Witherspoon. I think we can all call this one a closed case. Don't you?"

Part of me said to let it go, that it was foolish to butt heads with the likes of this man, who was obviously in cahoots with Hallett and who knows who else. But I was tired of everyone pushing me aside. I had felt like letting go of everything of late, just not caring anymore, running off, maybe even joining Dillinger's gang themselves, before the big guy got rubbed out. Taking a stand could be dangerous but no more so than doing nothing and dying without really knowing who you were any more.

"I've got a man that no one seems to want to acknowledge. A drunken man, hopped up on his own sense of importance, willing to shoot a policeman. We don't get that kind of man around here much, Mr. Childers. I aim to find out who he was."

That grip on my shoulder got a little tighter. "You do what you have to do. Be careful the road you're on doesn't lead to a dead end."

I heard it. The emphasis was on *dead*, as in that's where I'd wind up. The thing he didn't know, the thing that no one knew, was that Baron Witherspoon was already dead.

Chapter Eighteen

I was alone and I knew it. It was the same as when I went to war until I met at least one good friend. The same as when I came home not knowing if I would be accepted or if I fit in. Those times it just took a while for everything to work out. This was different. I had always been leery of big money men like Childers, or slimy politicians like Hallett. I'd seen enough of them as a kid. But not knowing about Chief Taylor, not feeling like he'd be able to bail me out of a jam was something that tightened up my insides. He was the one who guided me along all these years, in essence teaching me how to be a policeman and what it meant to serve others. This sudden feeling of abandonment was overwhelming.

Maybe all these years I had become too comfortable in my skin, laying back and waiting for the other shoe to fall, not intending to do anything other than let enough time pass to make everything seem okay. When that happens, you don't know who you are any more, and you don't rightly care.

The problem was that I did care. People like Beth Handy and her dad, good old guys like Big Ray and George, Mrs. McGuire. I cared about the people who would give you the shirt off their back and bring you soup if you were sick. It was nothing I had growing up but now it meant something to me. It meant just about everything. Caring that much made me dangerous to those who didn't.

I hung around the packing plant for a few days, never seeing Jack Hale or his car. On a hunch, considering my meeting with Martin Childers and the fact I didn't trust him as far as I could toss a stone, I ambled by Kanotex. I saw Hale's car but I was never able to catch him coming or going. It was apparent he changed positions and was now associated in some fashion with Childers. At this point, I wasn't certain which of the two was more dangerous.

I was able to sneak in a back entrance of the Gladstone when a housekeeping lady stepped out to beat a rug. I walked up the back stairs and roamed the corridors on several floors keeping my eyes and ears open for anything. I wasn't sure what I was looking for considering I didn't know the lady's name. Suddenly, an idea popped into my head.

In the lobby, I found an envelope with the hotel's address on it. I pulled a piece of paper from my notepad and scrawled *We need to talk. Moran.* I folded the paper in half, stuffed it in the envelope, and licked it shut. On the front, I wrote *Jack Hale* and then placed it on the counter. I sat down in a chair in the lobby, then stood up all official-like when Phil Garmes came down from the upper floors. He noticed the envelope before he saw me moving toward him. He turned his back on me and quickly placed the envelope in the slot for 2B. When he turned around, he acted surprised to see me. "Officer Witherspoon."

"You heard about the shooting?"

"I did."

"What did you hear?"

"Well, that you shot a drunk in self-defense." His response was too quick and too planned, almost like an actor quoting a well-rehearsed line from a play.

"Did you know him?" I knew to keep the questions coming quickly. For one thing, it might be easier to get Phil to slip up and tell me something he hadn't planned to. But it would always keep him from thinking about the envelope and how it got there.

"Well, he wasn't staying here, so..."

"Yeah, but did you know him?"

"No, officer, I didn't." His tone of politeness and courtesy was sounding strained, as though I had scraped the varnish off him and was exposing his rawness and all his flaws.

"How many people you suppose you get staying here from up north?"

"North, like...Canada?" He knew what I meant and was trying to rankle me as much as I appeared to be getting to him.

"Like Chicago."

"Couldn't say. The hotel doesn't require guests to identify where they're from."

"If you had to guess?"

"This isn't the midway at Arkalalah. Guessing won't win me any prizes. And Mother Garmes didn't raise no foolish sons."

There wasn't much more to say. I felt like Phil who had been a penny-ante hustler had recently stepped up into the big time but was obviously not cut out for it. I was hoping I could get to him before they did. He didn't realize how useless you could get pretty quick and make yourself worthless and expendable.

For now, I knew where Mr. Hale was located in

terms of living and working. I could focus on those areas and determine how he spent his time. There was no use in determining who else he might be involved with, or if any others like him were around. I had to assume there were more. Things had started to change since he came to town. That made him the tipping point.

As I left, I saw Councilman Hallett coming down the sidewalk seemingly heading for the hotel. Our eyes met. He paused for the briefest of moments. Perhaps he was planning on visiting Mr. Hale or someone else. Perhaps he was looking for me. It appeared for a moment he didn't want to do either. He proceeded with vigor toward me, calling my name. "I am having Dr. Brenz prepare a full report for your file."

"That's mighty nice of you."

"Officer Witherspoon, I want to make one thing perfectly clear. This has nothing to do with being nice. This incident has roused a lot of feathers among the other members of the council. Whereas public safety is our top priority, they do not want to consider that a member of our police department might think of himself as one of the members of the Dalton gang." I opened my mouth to protest but he continued. "I felt the best course of action was an expedient judgment. The fact that it was favorable to you should be cause for relief."

"I appreciate your delicate handling of this." It was his turn to be cut off by me. I wouldn't let him continue on the offensive. "However, it's our job to conduct the proper investigations. We can't have other people doing our jobs, now can we, Councilman? Then we'd wind up like the Wild West all over again. What we need is law and order. Isn't that right, sir?" I tipped my hat and turned away.

Two times I had been leaned on by bigwigs trying to convince me to stay out of something that darn near got me killed. There was no way I could forget it. By checking out Dr. Brenz's report, I'd be able to determine just how alone I was.

Chapter Nineteen

Jake left Kanotex shortly before all the real workers. He spent the biggest portion of his day in a large conference room provided by Martin Childers perusing news clippings and looking carefully over maps of the area. They covered Kansas, Oklahoma, Arkansas, and Missouri. On brown butcher paper he had scrawled notations regarding banks, their sizes, their prospective take. Whereas Childers was content with the steady income of the local area, Hickey was able to convince him to expand his range. This allowed for a bigger take and more control. He had quickly proven his skill at this to a bunch of rubes that stood gape-jawed and dumb-founded most of the time. It didn't take long to figure if a blustery fool like Martin Childers could run this burg, he'd be taking it over in no time. For now, he was only an employee and had many jobs to do.

Getting back to the hotel early, he hurried through the lobby until Phil Garmes called to him. "This came while you were out."

Phil handed Jake the envelope. He tore into it and shook like a kid at a birthday party. The note made his face light up for the first time in forever. "When did this come?"

"Sometime this afternoon."

"Who delivered it?"

"I don't know."

"What do you mean you don't know?"

"I was in the back room, then I came out, and this envelope was on the front counter. It was right before that nosy cop showed up."

"Which one?" Jake was on the verge of an epileptic fit. His glee at getting a note from George Moran was being undermined by the possibility it was all a twisted trick.

"Witherspoon. The one who was involved in the shootout last night."

Jake crumbled the note in his hand, like it was just so many stale animal crackers. He wasn't willing to accept the fact that a hick cop from the sticks in Kansas was making trouble for him. Jake knew police captains in Chicago who'd line up a poker game for him and provide protection. This level of disrespect was something he was not used to experiencing.

Heather wasn't in the room, which sent Jake into a tizzy. He walked down the stairs with loping strides, stomping the steps like a herd of buffalo. The only place he could think to go was the millinery. As he entered, his head swiveled in every direction as though he were scoping out a machinegun nest. Beth approached him with polite caution, trying not to spook him.

"Can I help you?" she asked, her voice almost a whisper.

"Uh, yeah, I'm…looking for…"

"Your wife?"

It took Jake a moment to recall the story and the part he was playing. Then, like a good actor, a calm came over him and he smiled. "Yes."

"She was here earlier and said she had more shopping to do."

"That's fine." He looked her over as though measuring her for a coffin, thinking this sweet piece of cornbread was something special to that pain in the ass cop. "You like living here?" he inquired politely.

"It's my home."

"But do you like it?"

"Well, sure. It's quiet and peaceful and safe."

Jake smiled with a geniality reserved for a true gentleman. He kept from appearing like a circus clown. These people were a flock of sheep, bleating in unison. They had a vision of their world seen only through rose-colored glasses. They had no idea what a man like him was capable of doing to that world.

When he got back to the room, Heather was listening to the radio, the daily newspaper tossed on the bed. "Where were you?" he blurted.

"Shopping."

"You weren't at that hat store."

"There are other places in this town to shop. Took me a while to find them."

Jake washed his face and hands, combed his hair, then peeled a double sawbuck off his roll. "Grab some dinner for yourself tonight. Make it something nice."

"What about you?"

"Got a meeting."

She pouted like a puppy that got swatted on its nose.

"When I get back, you can show me how much you love me." He winked, tipped his hat, and left just as quickly as he came into the room.

He was told to meet at the flower shop five blocks

further south on Summit. Just the thought of a flower shop reminded him of Deanie O'Banion. Poor guy died doing the thing he loved, cut down by Torrio's hired guns. Then there was Hymie and the Schemer. It got ugly for a while until George took over and everything seemed to be okeydokey. That was before Torrio got cold feet and ran home to Pastaville and let that fat Wop run things into the ground. Jake had it good for a while. George trusted him and could count on him. Unfortunately, that got the attention of every greaseball with a Chicago typewriter. George knew that if the North Side gang were going to survive, he would need Jake. This quaint little store with a small counter and a smaller back room still reminded him of the guys who guided him throughout his life and now seemed to be distant memories.

The tall slender man known as Dietrich, nodded at Jake, instructing him to follow. In the back room, a rough-sewn throw rug was pulled back revealing a kind of door in the floor with a ring to pull it open. The stairs were steep but there was some kind of light below. Jake led the way while Dietrich followed.

The tunnel was narrow at first and then expanded. A string of light bulbs ran down the middle, just above Jake's head; Dietrich had to constantly duck. Boarded up doors appeared every so often on either side. Jake looked back at Dietrich. "What's in there?"

"Used to be hoochie-coochie rooms back in the day."

Jake could not imagine bedding a girl in the cold underground.

Several yards further into the tunnel, an opening without a door led to a large room, which was about the size of a small juice joint. A long bar with a brass foot rail stood along one side and teased with thoughts of dolled-up dishes getting blottoed on hooch. When they repealed Prohibition, it put a lot of bootleggers on the dole.

The majority of the room contained stacks of wooden cases labeled as Canadian whiskey. Three other men with their jackets off and their sleeves rolled up, were carrying the cases out the other side of the room where another opening led to a hand cart on a mini rail track.

"What gives?" Jake was only told he was needed for the night but not what the game was.

"This was a shipment hijacked from Joplin right before Repeal come around. Now it's not worth a warm cup of spit. Mr. Childers has a friend with a nightclub in Dallas. We're loading a truck to sell it to him. Hey, it cost us nothin', we're still ahead."

Dietrich had a nasally laugh with a high-pitch that made him sound like a congested hyena. He stopped just as quickly. He was more about finishing a job than cracking wise.

Working alongside these men, Jake felt like a potato farmer in County Cork. He had worked his way through the rackets in Chicago, been sent away for safety's sake, and had made a splash in the dribs and drabs of Kansas. He needed to make a move and be the one shelling out the assignments instead of taking them.

The guy next to him shot a glance, then looked a little closer. He had a sad face that drooped like an old bloodhound with the same sagging eyes.

"You from Chicago, right?"

"Yeah. Hickey. Jake Hickey."

"Crazy Jake?"

Jake smiled. He had spent so long trying to remember he was someone. Now a complete stranger reminded him. "That's right."

"Pat McArdle." They shook hands like gentlemen.

"You were one of Frankie Gusenberg's guys?"

"Yeah." Those eyes were on the verge of tears. Jake knew the memory of St. Valentine's Day still bothered a lot of guys, himself included. "Did some work for Billy Skidmore after that. Almost felt like I was goin' legit."

"How long you been down here?"

"Two months, give or take. You?"

"Longer. Still waiting to hear from George."

"You mean Bugs Moran?"

"Yeah."

"If he's your meal ticket home, you're going hungry, fella."

Jake turned suddenly, grabbed McArdle by the shirt, and pushed him hard up against a stack of cases, the bottles rattling. Dietrich came back into the room, started forward until McArdle shook him off. "What do you mean?"

"The syndicate has pushed him out. He don't control nothin' no more. Last I heard he was knocking over a juke joint outside of the city limits."

Jake's eyes burned with heat. Snot was coming out of his nose. He looked like a bull in a corrida. His breathing had started to subside. He let go of McArdle, stepped back, and did everything he could to calm down. He went back to loading crates, working harder and faster than the other three men. When it appeared they were done, he grabbed his jacket, rebuttoned his shirtsleeves, and put his jacket back on, almost forcing his arms into the sleeves. Without waiting for further instructions from Dietrich, he walked out the way he came, back up the ladder, and out into the street through the floral shop.

Deanie O'Banion and the North Side gang were now part of history. Jake determined he would not follow suit.

Chapter Twenty

I needed something to calm me down, give me a sense of connection with anything human and real and honest. I needed to be around Beth Handy. In all honesty, I didn't know her as well as she thought I did or should have. I didn't know anyone that well, not even myself. When I came back from the war, I was starting over, literally. Everything that came before was a distant memory, basically a story I had been told, with nothing to put my finger on and know for sure was real. I was completely disconnected, like floating free in a hot-air balloon. I had never before wanted to be a part of something. Oh, maybe I'm telling tales just a bit. I guess when I was younger, it was important to be part of a group or a gang. Your pals could save your neck. Sometimes they'd wind up getting it in a noose.

I usually didn't walk right into the millinery. Most times I would just pass by and tip my hat. It was about being coy and not leading Beth on into something I knew I couldn't be a part. Right now, I was needing to see that sweet smile and those puppy dog eyes. It was something that had nothing to do with hooch or gangsters or all the bad men of the world. When I walked in, I saw that Beth was with a lady customer who had her back to me. My eyes met Beth's and her smile was enough to make me feel as though I were a newborn baby, fresh and clean and untarnished.

The lady turned around as Beth stepped away. It was Jack Hale's wife. She saw me and her smile was bigger than Beth's, but for a different reason. The calm that had been created vanished like the dew on the grass. It appeared I would have to tackle this situation head-on.

"Hello, sheriff."

"It's *officer*, ma'am."

"I'm just teasing."

"I gathered that." I was smiling and I was friendly but I was none too happy, and I let it show in my tone. "I don't believe we actually met."

She extended her hand as if she were one of them swells from the Big City. I didn't mind playing the part of a knight in shining armor, so I took her hand but did not kiss it. She may have had more class than most anybody else in town but she was no Queen Victoria.

"Heather Devore."

"You're Mr. Hale's wife?"

She paused as though I was asking a question on a test.

"Yes. His...wife."

"You don't seem too sure."

"Are you married, officer?"

"No, ma'am."

"Don't let them fool you. Marriage is not always pie in the sky, and peaches and cream."

I smiled, sort of, and politely nodded. I didn't know what she meant because all the guys I knew who were married had pretty good lives. Then again, from what I'd seen of Mr. Hale, I guess she knew what she was talking about.

We stood there for a moment with her looking like

she wanted to say something but didn't know how.

"I heard there was a shooting the other night." Her voice had a touch of concern but it wasn't motherly. I was guessing she was not interested in being anyone's mother.

"Yes. A drunk pulled a gun on me."

"Oh, my. Were you injured?"

"No, ma'am."

"Does that happen often here?"

"No. Not like it does in, say, Chicago."

"It can be dangerous anywhere. All it takes is a match against a powder keg."

I wasn't all too sure if Hale was the match or the powder keg. Fortunately, Beth came over with a box wrapped with ribbons and handed it to Ms. Devore like it was a rare jewel.

"Can you put that on my account, dear?"

I'm sure Beth didn't mind being called dear when it was just the two ladies in the store. But she got that look in her eye like a bratty little child who held her breath till she turned blue. This time, Beth's smile seemed painted on her face. I started to turn to leave, thinking this was not a good time, when Ms. Devore grabbed my arm with a soft touch as though she afraid of hurting me. "Could we speak? Privately?"

We walked just down the street, stepping into a hardware store. It seemed an odd place for a conversation between the two of us.

"My...husband is not doing as well as he thought he would."

"How so?"

"His idea in coming down here was to work hard and live a little less cheaply...well, no offense." I nodded for her to continue. "You can imagine how much it costs to live in the city, especially in these times. Well, by coming here, he felt it would be easier to make some money so we could continue on with the lifestyle we had before."

"And that's not the case?"

"No. I see him getting more and more frustrated and angry."

"You know, Ms. Devore, maybe he ought to start thinking about a different lifestyle. I've known a lot of happy people here. Life can be real good, if you don't set your expectations too high."

Her smile turned into one I'd seen on a chanteuse back in the war. It was designed to let you know that a woman was smiling, a woman who could remind you how good it felt being a man. It wasn't the dainty smile of an innocent farm girl. That one smile reminded me of the difference between her and Beth Handy

"Well, I might have something to do with that. You see, I don't want this kind of living. I want to get back to the kind of life I'm used to. I could never get used to this, well, small town life. Look at me. You see what I mean, don't you?" Her intention was to have me look at her body. It was a body that was meant for silks and perfumes and loving. I chose to be the smart catfish in the lake and avoid the bait.

I wasn't about to start doling out marital advice, especially in light of the fact I wasn't married. Yet, I did understand her. When I first got here, it was hard for me as well. The war, the different kind of women in France, their attitude and the things they could do and were willing to do. Then, shy and quiet and demure is what you're forced to accept. In my case, I figured it was something I had to do to survive. That may not have been as important for someone like Heather Devore who had the physical resources to achieve her desires. It was this place and Jack Hale that were holding her back.

"Well, I'm sorry it ain't working out too well. Seems to be pretty tough all over for most folks."

"I'm just afraid he might, well, I don't know what he would do. Perhaps he might get desperate."

"How desperate?" I didn't really have to ask. If what I suspected was true, this Jack Hale was already involved with things that would make the Old West outlaws look tame. She stepped closer to me, as close as she could get without actually touching me. I felt her warm breath cover me like a wool blanket on a winter's night when she spoke.

"At times, I'm afraid for my safety. As an officer of the law, that should concern you."

"It does." I was starting to feel a few other things concerning me. One was the idea of this extremely attractive woman being this close and this available to a man whose face was the furthest thing from Clark Gable there could be. It made me feel alive in a way that I hadn't felt for so long. After a moment, I remembered being the ghoul on Halloween, the guy that a dame like this would not turn her head for under normal circumstances.

"All I'm asking is that you keep an eye out for me. That's not too much to ask, is it?"

The wetness of her lips looked like a quiet lake that I wanted to jump into. In that brief moment I was willing to give up what I had become over the last sixteen years and return to the devil-may-care hard nose that I was. I stopped short of pulling off the mask.

"No, ma'am. It's not." The country boy was back in place. Now, he was being asked to take on the city slicker.

Chapter Twenty-One

Jake Hickey had never known what it was like to be on his own, completely without a gang or a crew or a leader with vision. Perhaps when he was young and his parents were dirt poor just like their potato-farming kin in Ireland. He might have had nothing but at least he had his family. Then there were the kids in the neighborhood and an offshoot of the Market Street Gang, being a slugger. Getting noticed by Deanie and taken under George's wing. He always knew he would never be alone. Certainly not when it came to women. Heather was another in a long line of tomatoes, another butter and egg fly. Only this one stayed around longer. Knew how to shut up when needed and when to start pitching woo. But now it seemed that George was no more, the gang was all broken up by the Big Syndicate and he was swirling in the farmlands of Kansas just waiting for a twister to completely tear his world apart. Being alone wasn't as cracked up as some guys made it out to be.

From what little he had seen, Childers seemed to have a handle on the action in the area but he got the impression he wasn't holding the strings. There were only a few guys from Chicago that he met. Some of these other lackeys were either local or from another part of the country, probably close by like Oklahoma City, Dallas, or Kansas City. They were holding on to their piece of the pie now that Prohibition was over. There would always be something to get into although this didn't seem like much of an area for the bawdy houses and farmers weren't all that excited by the numbers. The bigger cities were close enough. He just might be able to convince a few of these yokels to join him, branch out, or take over the whole shebang, run it the way he knew he could.

All along though, there was the cop, the one with the mangled face like he was hiding behind a mask. In spite of that, there was just something about him that seemed familiar, although he never knew how it could be possible. He figured the cop was on his tail, trying to make a play for Jake's action. The problem was, he didn't know if the cop was part of the crew on the take. Bagmen didn't look the same down here like they did on the North Side. One thing was for sure: based on that shootout, the cop was well acquainted with his gun and wasn't afraid about using it.

Jake was taking a walk along Summit, passing the movie house and watching the folks filter in for the show. The sky was clear and the stars were out forming their quaint mythological characters. He vaguely recalled his mother identifying the constellations and telling Jake the story of each. He was polite by letting her go on but it didn't mean that much to him. Gods and goddesses with lightning bolts and snakes. Heck, give him a tommy-gun any day of the week and twice on Sunday.

He just stood there, one hand in his pocket, the other easing a drag off a cigarette. He hadn't noticed that Officer Witherspoon was two feet from him looking up at the same sky.

"Any of them you recognize?" the cop asked, politely.

"Nah. I forgot that stuff as fast as I learned it. I was just wondering if the sky looks the same in Chicago as it does here."

"Lincoln Park, right?" Jake turned to face Witherspoon directly.

"So, how do you know it so well? I figure we're about the same age only I don't remember you. Guess it could be the scars."

Jake didn't really concern himself with being polite in return.

"A friend of mine. A guy I knew in the war."

"Yeah? What was his name?"

"Kimble. Eric Kimble."

Just as he did in Chicago when he and George had heard about the massacre, he kept his cool, didn't let on anything. He knew Kimble from the old days, a raucous and rambunctious kid. Petty theft mostly, a few apples and such, never cut out to be a slugger. Jake tried to get him in the gang but Kimble wouldn't have it. It's not that he wanted to be a priest or, worse yet, a cop. He seemed to care just a little bit more than the guys who got in. Maybe he didn't want to disappoint his mother.

Deanie took a shine to him, thought him to be an upstanding Catholic with a good heart. He protected Kimble from the other members of the Market Street Gang when they wanted to rough Kimble up, force him to decide one way or another which side to choose. O'Banion was like a proverbial older brother and saw that Chicago held no future for him. It was he who suggested joining the Army after hearing that other great Mick, George M. Cohan, belt out "Over There" and cause the hairs on the back of his neck to sizzle with patriotism, something Jake never had any use for.

"So, you two were friends?" Jake said it but didn't believe it.

"Well, you know, Mr. Hale, we were there a lot longer than we expected. Until you see a buddy choke his guts out on mustard gas, that's when you realize that all the guys were your friend no matter what their background was. It's something you might not understand."

Jake didn't take it as a slight considering how matter-of-fact the cop spoke it. "And he talked about Lincoln Park?"

"We both talked a lot about where we were from. He made the city sound pretty exciting. I guess I talked a lot about the people around here and how special they were to me. I think he just might have followed me back here if he'd have lived."

Just when Jake thought he had a handle on this guy, he got thrown a curveball. Eric Kimble was dead and all of this was just a guy rehashing his friend's stories. Jake had to know for sure just how much this cop knew. "He mention me at all?"

"I don't rightly recall. It was a long time ago. I just remember a guy who was willing to make a big change to find some peace in his life. I suppose anyone could if they wanted to."

There it was: the schoolboy lesson. The whole thing was some cornball come-on, a little trick of a story, a moral from a tale to be told. He was starting to realize how typical these laid back, church going Kansans were with their sense of living a good, clean life. Witherspoon might have just as well said, "It would be so easy for you and your lady to settle down and start a new life and not let the past get a hold of you."

All that *Ragged Dick* and *Oliver Twist* stuff. Bad boy makes good. Rags-to-riches. Only Jake wasn't seeing a lot of riches in simply working himself for eight to ten hours a day so Heather could have a home and a garden and a white picket fence.

"We all have our own dreams, Officer Witherspoon."

"I suppose so." Baron half smiled and nodded and turned to walk off.

"How'd he die?"

Baron turned back. His face went blank, sagged a bit, eyes recessing into painful memories.

"A small patrol of Krauts, well, Germans, ran into us and we started running. Shells were pouring down from all around. We had gotten lost so we had no idea who was bombing us. We were just nearing one of our trenches. Eric kept yelling at us to run. He had just pushed me in when a shell exploded right behind him. The force was so hard it threw him on top of me." Baron stopped, looked down at his feet, and was doing everything he could to hold back a tear. "I won't ever forget that."

Just then, it was as though Baron was an inner tube and someone began pumping him back up. The color came back to his face. His shoulders were upright and squared. He had returned to the moment, the quiet and peaceful moment of a small town in Kansas after having taken a brief journey to madness and dirt and death and Hell. He turned and walked away

Jake would have to go around Witherspoon or

through him. He presented himself as a man of simple resolve, wanting nothing more than to keep the tiller steady against the impending storm. What Jake had seen too many times before was an explosion from those who had something buried inside. Had Jake not been around, this Witherspoon might live a good long life to a ripe old age. Unfortunately, Jake Hickey now called Ark City his home, and two men of the same ilk would not be able to co-exist. Jake knew he'd have to be the one to light the fuse.

Chapter Twenty-Two

Chief Taylor came from a long line of oil men in
and around Tulsa. His father had been a wildcatter from
as far back as he could remember and instilled the
adventurous sense of "boom or bust" in his son. It
wasn't much of a stable life but it sure was interesting.
Word was his family knew Arthur Floyd's family; some
say even broke bread together. People whispered that,
in recent times, he might have looked the other way
when Floyd was somewhere in the area, like he was
back in '32. Before that, he followed in his father's
footsteps. When the wells ran dry and his luck ran out,
he got into law enforcement. He had a no-nonsense
attitude about him, which is what I liked best. It didn't
seem to make much sense to me to act like you were on
a vaudeville stage when you were a policeman. You
always knew where you stood with him. That didn't
necessarily make things easier, just more honest was
all.

His wife was a country girl through and through.
Irma thought nothing of waking up before dawn and
baking bread and milking cows and feeding pigs. It was
this hard work sensibility that kept Chief Taylor on a
farmstead outside of town. He would never cotton to a
fancy home right in the city. I think it allowed him to
break away from all the muck and grime that went
along with his job. It was far cleaner out there.

It wound up being the perfect place for me to go and report. Unless I was being followed, it would provide a degree of privacy that was necessary. Of course, if I were being followed, I'd know exactly who it was.

He was chopping wood for his wife's stove. Shirtless, suspenders holding up his pants, and sweating enough to fill the Red Sea, he seemed entirely different—like a man who had better things to do in life than catch criminals.

"Glad you could come out, Baron."

"No problem at all, sir."

"Irma," he yelled back inside the house. "Bring out some lemonade."

I waited until Mrs. Taylor had come and gone to pull out my notebook and pass along the information I had. The last thing I wanted to do was to intrude upon her courtesy.

"I've got a Jack Hale who came down from Chicago a little over a year ago. Started working at Keefe and LeStourgeon but now is over at Kanotex."

"You know what he does?"

"Nothing as far as I can tell. His car is outside the plant every day like a working man. Only thing is I haven't been able to tell is what kind of work he does."

"How do you know he's from Chicago?"

"I talked to him."

His eyebrow raised pretty high, kind of like those nuns back when I was growing up. You said the wrong thing, you got the look followed by a mean swat.

"A couple of times," I continued. "Once in Junior's and then just recently outside the movie house."

"What makes you think he doesn't know you're on

to him?"

I closed my notebook for a moment and had the feeling I was talking to a raw rookie who had never walked a night patrol before. "He knows. Just like Martin Childers knows. The people that run the bad stuff in this town don't aim to make it all that much of a secret."

He looked tense, like he was holding back a scream. Just the implication that someone other than law and order and elected officials were running the town rubbed him the wrong way. The thing I was starting to see was it was the police and elected officials who were running things, both the good and the bad. You were either in or ran the risk of getting run over.

"Nobody's doing anything out in the open at least." By him saying that it was supposed to make things better.

"Not here. Not that we know of. But what about them bank jobs a while back, just all around us? Seems a little strange it should be everywhere but here."

"That's what we were thinking."

"You got a North Sider from Chicago who's basically cut off from his world. You got the local bigwigs looking for a gunsel who can take orders and has some experience. The syndicate hadn't made it this far south yet. These guys can take advantage of what's left for a while."

"What makes you think some other gangster won't come riding into town and raise a ruckus and cause some kind of war?"

He did have a point. Somewhat. "Hardly anyone left. The police shot down Homer Van Meter in Minnesota last month. All you got left is Nelson and

Floyd. Nelson's too much of a hothead. But, Floyd, he could be trouble."

"Arthur Floyd won't give anyone any trouble." He said it fast, like he was coming to his brother's defense. Maybe he knew Pretty Boy or maybe he just had a different feeling about him. "Who else do we have to worry about?"

"This Hale has got a dame. She makes herself out to be his wife…"

"They all do."

"I got the feeling she wants out and she's looking for a new meal ticket."

"What makes you say that?"

"She told me her *husband* might do something desperate."

"Putting the finger on him." He nodded. He took a cloth from his back pocket, wiped his head and face, then turned his gaze toward the sky for a spell. Perhaps he was waiting for divine guidance. I would be, too, if I had any faith in it. I was certain there was something hot brewing in the pot and we needed to get ahead of it before a lot of innocent people got killed.

"You need to locate a man named Abram Dutcher," the chief said.

"Who is he?"

"Used to run things many years ago. An old German Jew. They called him *Der Kaiser.* Got pushed out around the time you went off to fight the Hun. No one, not even the shady businessmen, could accept a German running things while our boys were in the trenches. A lot of 'em felt it was bad for business."

"What happened to him?"

"He disappeared for a while. Wound up resurfacing

about ten years later. Kept his hand in the till just enough to get a small piece of the action. Ran a house in Joplin. Girls, gambling, booze."

"How do you know about this?" I asked, innocently. Chief Taylor smiled. The cagey old cop still had a few tricks up his sleeve and knew better than to give away all his secrets. "So, where do I find him?"

"Start asking. He'll find you."

"And when he does?"

He came toward me, putting his hands on my shoulders, acting like a father even though he was only about fifteen years or so older. He was sending me into the lion's den and was worried about it. The thing he didn't know was that I wasn't.

"He'll help you dig deep, Baron. I'm sure there's nothing he'd like better than to see the men that pushed him aside get their due. But don't get me wrong. This won't be free and it won't come cheap. You're going to owe him. I don't know, it may even get you in hot water with the force. I know what I'm asking but if we don't stop it here, this town won't be a decent enough place to live anymore."

I understood him. Clearly. It takes a trash man to clear away the junk and litter. It's a thankless job but it keeps things neat and clean. I had come to the realization that everything from my past was being swept aside and this, right here, was what I was meant to do. Maybe it was my destiny. Who knows? I had no desire to be a hero or wear medals. Just like the war, the only goal was to survive and make it home safely. Whether it was the battalion or Mr. Handy and Beth or Mrs. McGuire, there were people who only wanted to live their lives and have a little comfort. This wasn't the

Argonne Forest or a battle zone, and I couldn't let it get that way.

I understood Chief Taylor completely. If I was to die doing it, then maybe Fate was coming back from sixteen years before to make me pay the bill. Either way, I was going to do everything possible not to let Jack Hale and the rest take over. And it started with finding Abram Dutcher.

Chapter Twenty-Three

The thought of being something other than yourself is a bit daunting. I know what my morals are, and the difference between good and bad. I've chosen this path, that of a police officer. I am certain, without actual knowledge, that there are some on the Ark City police force who have been paid to look the other way when illegal or questionable things are happening. I've talked to many who thought prohibition was wrong, that a man had a right to a drink all the way back to the Bible. I wasn't one to agree or disagree. When it was the law, I had to enforce it.

Now, I had to make my way into the confidence of men who may not have been so much different than me. We all put our pants on the same way. They just had a different notion on how to earn a dollar. I don't mind admitting I was scared, not for my safety but for a lack of success. Childers and Hallett, and who knows who else were already aware of my stance. It would be difficult to convince them I turned completely around, out of the blue. My only chance was to determine some of the other low level mobsters and squeeze them for info.

I still had no idea how to pull Abram Dutcher out of the woodwork. Perhaps if I just started asking around, like poking a stick in a snake hole, I might get some movement. There was a possibility of getting bit as well. I had never heard of him before, and I thought it was dangerous to try to conjure up a demon from the past. It was Chief Taylor who felt I needed to make his acquaintance as though he could help pull back the curtain on the whole charade.

Junior's was the place to go. There wouldn't be any bigwigs there, just the working class grunts who wanted to blow off steam. I had met Ms. Devore and Mr. Hale there so it was a safe bet. It seemed strange when I felt myself puffing out my chest and feeling like I could take on the world when I entered. It was as though I were on stage or maybe just reverting to old ways.

No one gave me a second look. I was accepted there because the owners said so. It might just as well have been because they didn't feel the police were smart enough to figure out their play or powerful enough to do anything about it. I knew for a fact they weren't so smart themselves. They were tougher and didn't care. Life and death was meaningless to them, both their opponents' and their own. People around these parts admired Charlie Floyd, calling him the "Robin Hood of the Cookson Hills." That was just sad Okie talk. During the troubled times, the banks were the bad guys, the enemies, taking away homes and farms. Most didn't realize they were just doing their jobs. So when stories come out that Charlie is burning mortgages and destroying papers while he's robbing these banks, it kind of made him out to be a hero. The truth was he stole and killed. That's not a hero in anyone's book, unless someone else is reading it to you.

I saw a table with three men I hadn't seen before, either here or in town. They sat smoking and drinking and talking quietly which was odd for a juke joint when most people were acting loud and brassy. I was about to dismiss them from my thoughts when Jack Hale and Heather Devore came in not looking ready for a party. The other men livened up by his appearance; Ms. Devore looked bored. Our eyes met and she smiled.

Jack pulled up a chair for himself and called over to the bartender to get another round for the table. One of the men got up and offered his chair to the lady, who seemed to be just standing there. I wasn't sure if Jack saw me or even cared. We had met and spoke and were quite clear on where each other stood. That would be enough for now.

She leaned over to talk to the man next to her. It was either too loud for him to hear or she was trying to get intimate because she was real close to his ear. The man who gave her his chair and was now standing leaned down to join in the conversation.

Jack looked up from his conversation. He gave her a blank look. His eyes rose further and caught mine. He returned to his conversation.

The black piano player was playing stride style. He looked like he was hopped up on something. There was a big white-toothed smile on a face that was covered with sweat.

A redheaded B girl floated up behind me. Her hand landed on the soft part of my backside. I turned my head slightly. Everything about her said *Take me*.

"I'm Stephanie. I don't suppose you'd like to buy me a drink."

"I don't drink, Stephanie."

"Yeah, but I do."

I went back to looking straight ahead. She finally

figured I was a nut she couldn't crack.

Ms. Devore got up from her chair helped by the man who offered his seat. She walked slowly toward the stage, watched the piano player for a bit, and then stood at the end of the bar. Jack and the man he was talking with got up and left.

Behind me was a table with two old white-haired fuddy-duddies sipping whiskey and looking around at the attractive women. I was sure Stephanie hadn't made an appearance there.

"Mind if I join you gents?"

"You ain't drinkin'," said the bearded one. "Cain't trust a man who ain't got a drink."

"That's probably true." I motioned to the bartender who wound up bringing me a grape Nehi. "I got my drink." I smiled broadly.

"Well, I'll be damned and gone to hell." The bearded man smiled back. We clinked glasses.

We sat silently for a while. I didn't want to make it look so obvious that I was looking for information even though that's exactly what I was doing. I had learned a long time ago, further back than even the war, that you cannot underestimate an old codger. What they have lost in ability, they have made up in experience and knowledge.

"This much different than when you were young?" I asked politely.

"Hell, yes," said the man with the thick sideburns.

"A lot more class back then," the bearded man chimed in.

"Was that on account of Der Kaiser?" I just threw it out there, like casual conversation, like we were all good friends who had shared a mutual history.

"Could be," said Sideburns with a little caution in his voice. "The man was no nonsense. Didn't believe in all this hullaballoo."

"That why he was pushed out?"

"That weren't it at all. He was a Kraut. We were at war with the Krauts. You of all people ought to know that."

They knew me enough to know my background even though I knew nothing about them. That had me worried a bit.

"Yes, sir. I do. Shame to lose a good man like that."

"He ain't lost, son," said the Beard, smiling and crinkling the wrinkles in his face. "He just ain't found."

Maybe that alone would send the message. Meanwhile, I casually observed Heather Devore floating around like a bee pollinating flowers, getting her cigarette lit, laughing with various men. Jack had still not returned, and I couldn't be sure if he was going to come back any time soon. She never looked at me again for the remainder of the night. I thought she might be hedging her bets and seeking out an alternative if I didn't come through for her.

An elderly gentleman stood at the bar as she passed, but I continued following her movements. When I looked back again, he was gone. It seemed as though he were looking at me, or at least in my direction. I decided it was this place doing it to me, making me have visions, trying to make me remember times long forgotten. If I kept on this path, it would all come back to me. That had me more afraid than anything.

Chapter Twenty-Four

It was in one of those side rooms, the ones Dietrich referred to as the hoochie-coochie rooms, where they met. A dusty wooden table and five rickety chairs sitting on a dirt floor with a stench of mustiness weren't even close to the appearance of a high-end conference room in a swanky hotel in Chicago. Jake had already learned things weren't like they were in the Windy City and were never going to be. Dietrich was there, getting tired of being a wet nurse with no future, getting no trust and respect from Childers. Pat McArdle showed up. He had the same feeling as Jake. It was much too good back in the big city, and he just wasn't willing to let go of a good thing and settle for less. Jimmy O'Donnell was the youngest brother of the South Side O'Donnells. He was a half brother from his father's affair with a cigarette girl in a small nightclub, but Spike acknowledged him as a full brother. He was barely sixteen when big brother Spike survived a machine gun attempt on his life. He gave Jimmy a pocketful of cash and told him to go anywhere but Chicago. Jimmy didn't have the criminal sensibilities of his brother and drifted until he wound up in Kansas. The last man was Sean Brennan, originally from Milwaukee but did some work for Hymie Weiss. He could easily have been an actor in the pictures. Slick looking, well-groomed, clean-shaven, dark sinister eyes with a slight upturned smile. A little like Charles Farrell or Warner Baxter. There was no way of telling what was on his mind.

"There's enough here for all of us." Jake was feeling like the chairman of the board.

"In this burg?" It was Brennan that was voicing the doubts.

"Not here. All around us. I've got sources that tell me there are two banks, a jewelry store, and a fur store in three block area in a town just north of Dallas."

"What sources?"

Jake didn't mind being questioned when it came to a guy wanting assurance of a lucrative payout. However, he felt like Brennan was going to question him on everything. That was going to make for a lot of tension and cause Jake to question bringing this guy into the mix.

"I was on the truck with Childers' driver when we brought that hooch down there."

"I just don't want to be driving a couple of hundred miles for a bankroll won't last me a month."

Jake turned his attention back to the others.

"The take from the banks could be in the neighborhood of sixty-five to seventy-five thousand. The stuff from the jewelry and fur stores could be well over a hundred thousand. Naturally, we'll try to get the best return from a fence. It would still come out to be a decent payday for five guys forced to live in a one-horse farm town."

Brennan leaned forward, his eyes growing darker.

"Nobody's forcing me to live here."

Jake mimicked his posture, his eyes mirroring the darkness of Brennan, the special thing that made him

'Crazy' Jake starting to seep through his pores.

"You can go any time you'd like, Brennan. Take what pocket change you got from working for Childers and make your own mark." They stared at each other before Brennan realized he'd have to find another way around the fanatical gangster.

Dietrich's bass voice bounced off the stone walls, sounding like something out of a Biblical battle.

"We're going to have to be careful of Childers and Hallett. They've got eyes and ears all around."

Jake was surprised by the mention of the councilman. He wasn't aware of his involvement but had to cover this up so as not to allow these men to think he wasn't on top of the issue.

"The more successful we are, the more of their soldiers will come over to us. We can run things here if we just stick together."

Jake took a piece of stationery from the Gladstone on which he had written down the businesses in question. They were all within the vicinity of Red Brick Road in Richardson, Texas. The plan was to take two cars, have all the men dress well as though they were either businessmen or conventioneers. They would drive down the same route together but then each car would take a different route back, all of which Jake had outlined. They were to drive in shifts and not stop for the night. They were not to drive too fast. They were to meet back at this exact spot by a designated date and time.

"How you gonna find a fence for jewels and furs here?" Jimmy O'Donnell had learned a great deal from his brother, including being cautious as well as respectful. "Not only that, how are you gonna do that without Childers knowing?"

"Got a couple of guys I lined up in Wichita. They claim they can handle this kind of stuff and I believe them."

"Guys who claim to be able to handle merchandise. Banks and stores that could bring big cash. Lots of ifs and maybes for my liking." Brennan was sarcastic instead of aggressive now. But Jake was having none of that play. He knew he had figured this score out several times over to make it worthwhile. He felt Brennan was an add-on who could be dropped like a hot potato.

"Look, Brennan, you don't have to be a part of this if it don't suit you. You got a problem with it, take a walk. But if you stay, you keep that trap shut and follow what I tell you." Jake looked at each of them like a father handing down the law. It had to be a certain way to work. "The way I see it is we all got the bum steer. This was supposed to be a place to stay cool until the heat was off and we could all go back to what we knew. Well, that changed. The syndicate has pushed the mobs out, making them part of the history books. Our old gangs are gone. And we're sitting here on a deserted island with no one coming to our rescue. You want it that way, have it. Me, I still got plans I ain't willing to give up on. One thing's for sure. I am not taking orders from Childers or Hallett, or any other Kansas rube who thinks they know how to run an outfit. My goal is plain and simple: to get enough of a bankroll to pull out and go where skies are sunny and blue."

"You talkin' about Florida, Jake?" Pat's eyes sparkled like Christmas lights.

Yeah, Jake was thinking about Florida. Having been born and raised in Chicago, dealing with wind and cold and snow as well as the bright lights of the big city, he witnessed everything slowly working its way down the toilet. The old days were gone. George, wherever he was, was not coming to his aid, having to deal with his own problems. Who knows maybe this little side trip to Kansas saved him from falling on hard times and getting shot like a petty thug. He read the news articles about Homer Van Meter whose family said the poor bastard was used for target practice. Puffing out your chest and acting brave and tough wouldn't cut it any more. He needed cash, lots of it, to move on. Sure, he'd bring Heather with him. She'd look great in one of them bathing suits on the beach in Miami. Maybe she would stay looking like a hottie for a while and he wouldn't have to ditch her for a newer model. If he got bored, he could head on over to Cuba where they could use good men. It was ironic to consider Lucky Luciano and Meyer Lansky in some small way were pushing out the old mobs and Jake would even think about working for them. But that notion was a long way off.

"What comes after this Dallas thing?" Brennan sounded more like he was in step. There wasn't actually any eagerness in his voice. It was more like a cold sober determination.

"Oklahoma City. Then Kansas City. I'm working out the details." Brennan nodded in agreement. Jake was pleased. His small gang was ready to make a dent and fill their pockets. Now, it was a matter of keeping the heat off from the machine that was working in town. He stressed to the men to keep working their jobs, following the orders given, not complain about anything. He didn't want to alert Childers and his boys to anything off kilter. The Dallas job would take two days. Using various excuses, the five of them could be gone and back before anyone gave it any serious thought.

A smile came to him briefly. Witherspoon. Go ahead, copper, he thought. Follow me to Texas and back if you like. Jake was starting to care less and less about the lawman who had delusions of being his nemesis. Jake was the big fish in this small pond. No one was taking him down.

Chapter Twenty-Five

I had been working a little bit extra past my shift for several nights, reading newspapers and reports from the area, drawing circles and lines and arrows on a local map. For a while, it seemed awfully quiet, as though the shooting caused barely a hiccup in someone's plans. I didn't honestly think it was going to stop everything dead in its tracks. The people who ran things were smart enough to know when to keep quiet and lay low, long enough for the on-the-take guys and the noses-to-the-grindstone guys to let things blow over. It was the calmness that was most disquieting.

My mind kept going back to that night in Junior's when Heather Devore was floating around, like a stray puppy looking for table scraps. It was rather sad to think of her that way because she had the face and the body to grind men of stone into a fine powder. Perhaps where she came from it wouldn't have been that difficult. Down here she was a fish out of water fighting to keep herself stable and alive. As far as coming to her aid, I would certainly do so if it were a matter of the law. I knew I couldn't just drop almost sixteen years of being on the police force for a roll in the hay. I didn't know any gal worth that, and I'd had a few in my time.

Jack Hale was acting like a responsible citizen, going to his job at Kanotex, occasionally escorting Ms. Devore to dinner or the picture show, but very rarely going to Junior's. When someone like that is acting too good it's more than likely they're up to no good. Such an act might have played well at the Palace but I saw right through him.

My eyes felt like someone had poured lye into them, and my neck was tighter than a wingnut on a bicycle tire. Opening my eyes after screwing them up tight, the image of being stuck to that barbed wire popped up. Metal thorns jabbing into me no matter what direction I moved. Being stuck and not being able to get unstuck. A sharp cage fitting tighter than a straitjacket. It was the feeling of being trapped with no way out that kept coming back to me. It was the thing that Dr. Brenz was trying to get me to admit to, if not something else. I hadn't felt it that deeply in a long time. I was guessing it was due to what was happening right now, and I wondered if it would ever go away. Once you choose a direction, you might become trapped by it.

It was so late that no one's lights were on in downstairs parlors or upstairs windows. I came to my rooming house, which seemed to be enveloped in darkness. It was something I was used to. When I opened the door to my apartment and turned on the light, I saw him sitting there. He was an elderly man, just a bit older than Dr. Brenz, with grayish frizzled hair and a white goatee and moustache. He was dressed in a gray pinstripe suit with a white shirt and a perfectly knotted navy blue tie. His black shoes shined brighter than a pastor's on Sunday morning. His hands were folded neatly in his lap. Sitting in the dark seemed as natural to him as an owl on a tree branch at midnight.

The suddenness of his appearance caused me to

react by drawing out my gun and aiming it at him. I felt my eyes widen and a bead of sweat on my forehead while he sat nearly motionless.

"I am flattered you would think a man of my age could be considered dangerous enough to pull a gun on."

"This is my apartment and you don't live here. That's called Breaking and Entering."

A charming knowing smile appeared on his lips. "Or, if I had advised your landlady, Mrs. McGuire, that I was a dear old friend from the war, she might have allowed me access to wait until you arrived home."

The guy was playing cagey but he was right as well. Everyone was right: Just ask around for Der Kaiser and he'll find you. It was time to put away my gun. I wasn't sure if I had enough smarts to fight back.

"How may I help you, Officer Witherspoon?" The gracious tone was covering up a sinister element. He had complete control because it was obvious he knew more than I did, even though he had not been a presence in this town for as long as I'd come back from the war. It was wrong, however, to assume his experience was not as meaningful and his influence had waned. Not lost. Just not found. Until he wanted to be. I pulled up a chair from my small dining table and sat alongside him. It felt like I was at my dad's feet and there were to be stories told.

"I've got boys from Chicago down here. Seems like they may be putting together their own mob seeing as how the Syndicate has broken up all the old gangs. You read about it in the paper every day. Dillinger is dead, and his gang is almost gone. Capone's in jail, and Bugs Moran has just about been pushed out."

145

"How the mighty have fallen. But it was only a matter of time."

"What about the machine running this town?"

"Nothing like my day. These ne'er-do-wells have no style, no panache. Cheap criminals out to grab whatever they can."

"And how was it in your day?" I tried hard not to appear disrespectful, especially with a man I assumed had long been removed from the active criminal element in town. I had no way of knowing then that physical presence alone did not dictate true power.

"Politicians and businessmen worked at our behest, maintaining an environment conducive to financial gain. Because of that, they were able to provide well for the honest citizenry. Now, the elected officials have a notion to be in charge and employ hoodlums to steal from the masses. We offered private clubs with hostesses. They have juke joints and whores. Violence was used to resolve conflict, not to instill fear. I knew bosses who were able to retire and return to their homelands, whether it was Germany or Italy or Ireland. Many don't see forty today."

"Who am I up against, Mr. Dutcher?"

"The grandfather on the hill."

I had heard a variation on that expression countless times since I joined the force. I always thought it was a spook story, something to keep nosy cops away from the real forces behind the criminal element in town. A vague figure with no face. A being both real and unreal. But every once in a while, the Magnolia Ranch would pop into the conversation even though no one who had ever owned it was determined to be involved in any criminal activity. That either meant it was a tall tale or they were just too good at hiding themselves in the shadows.

"That doesn't give me much."

"Who do you think is running it all?"

"Childers owns the refinery. He's got money and the resources of men, probably a lot of them coming from Chicago."

"And what do you have on him?"

"Except for drinking whiskey in a dry state, nothing. He doesn't even leave town."

"Go higher."

"Hallett?"

"Who shut down the investigation into the man you shot?"

"You got a point. I just figured he wouldn't want to get his hands dirty."

"But you're not interested in past history, are you?"

"Not so much. I just get the impression there's a powder keg about to go off."

"You must be referring to Jake Hickey."

It felt like an anvil was dropped on my head. The name came out of nowhere faster than a freight train. All along I thought I was sparring with just another Irish North Sider, a slick boy named Jack Hale. I was too blind to see it was Jake Hickey. Too many years had passed for me to consider this twist of fate. I had forgotten him, partially due to my war experience and partly due to my trying to forget and leave all that behind me. I realized now it was foolish to tell him that story about Eric Kimble. He might have thought I was on to him earlier than now. With this assurance, I could figure out his plan.

Something must have happened to my face or my

expression because I felt frozen in time. Dutcher leaned forward and looked at me in a way my doctor would when he was concerned.

"Even though you did not know me, I was around before the war. I knew many many people. It's safe to say that a lot about you has changed." Since he had such a way with words, I couldn't tell what he was trying to get at.

"It's been a lot of years. I'm sure many of us have changed."

He stood up as graceful as a deer in a dewy meadow. He smoothed out his pants of creases and straightened his cuffs. It was as though an elegant leopard was going to saunter through.

"Childers and Hallett are not your concern. They are largely nothing more than businessmen who are willing to keep the peace as long as they maintain equity income. They have more to lose. Hickey is your problem. If he attempts to instill some sort of mutiny, there will be a bloodbath in the streets. Chicago is run by this Mafia. It's a highly sophisticated organization. You've heard of Charlie Luciano? They call him 'Lucky.' He would have no patience for a man like Jake Hickey. And neither should you."

He started to leave. I made a move to grab his arm and quickly realized how wrong it would have been. Clearing my throat worked just as well.

"I've got a lot to lose as well." For the first time in a long while, I could hear fear in my voice.

"You have to make a choice, Officer Witherspoon." He pronounced my name like it was a foreign word. "Whether to hold on to your past or ensure your future." I understood his meaning all too well.

"Where can I find you?"

"I'll be around. And I will find you."

The door opened and closed in almost total silence. The room seemed to lighten up a bit as though the darkness had emptied out. I knew who all the players were in this drama and what parts they were supposed to play. I just didn't have any idea what the next scene would be.

Chapter Twenty-Six

It was a long four days for Heather Devore. She was used to Jake going to his fake job to keep up appearances and spending a good portion of his evening doing something similar to what he did in Chicago. At least he was around to take her to dinner or a nightclub. She learned already that Junior's was the most decent place they had in town. If she felt like slumming there were at least half a dozen "private clubs" which were little more than watering holes serving rotgut gin that could strip wallpaper. They were usually frequented by hopheads and smelled of loss and decay.

At first it was odd going to bed without him at least in the room but she soon settled into a peaceful sleep and hoped this could last. The next day she went out, starting with pumping Phil Garmes for as much information as she could get: other types like Jake in town; rich men looking for soft female companions; an exit or a way out. All the slick kid could do was come on to her with nothing more than a tired line and stale breath.

She was vaguely aware Officer Witherspoon was somewhere around, perhaps watching over her. She imagined him wanting her, wanting to come and rescue her from the thug she had latched onto for no better reason than money and booze and a good time. Eventually, she guessed he was a goody two shoes and she was not going to be able to draw him into her clutches. It was a shame, but there were others in town.

It didn't matter to her if someone saw her at Junior's and reported it to Jake. He had any number of reasons for tanning her hide, drunk or sober. It was getting to a point where if she were going to use her womanly charms she needed to do it before Jake beat her beauty into a mass of bruises and welts, making her sex appeal worthless.

Regrettably, she had no success by the time he came back. He was in an overly jovial mood, just like years ago after he and Bugs and the boys hijacked a Capone liquor shipment or taking a shipping company's payroll. He was wound up and ready to Jitter Bug like the Cab Calloway song that just came out. He took her out to dinner that night at the best place in town stuffing food in his mouth so fast she thought he might explode.

"How's about we go on a little road trip? Kind of like a vacation."

"Where to?" she said suspiciously, an eyebrow being raised with a mix of passion and doubt.

"Wichita."

"What's there?"

He wiped his mouth with his napkin and tossed it onto the plate. He leaned forward so as not to raise his voice. "All right, look. I've got some business to take care of. I figured you ain't been outta this dump for a while. They got nice stores and better clubs. You can go shopping while I'm dealing with my stuff and then we can pretend like it's the old days."

Initially, there was a quiver in her chest. The thought of things being like they were had an excitement to it. Wichita, being a bigger city, would most certainly be more fun, nothing like Chicago but better than the sleepy little town she was stuck in. Maybe, she thought, Jake might be convinced to move there instead of staying in Arkansas City. Perhaps a small house instead of a hotel. Then she saw herself falling into a big pit called a pipe dream. This minor detour into fantasy starting to give her false hope that things could be better between her and Jake. She knew she had to stop allowing herself to think that way, and realize Jake was like a boiler that could blow any time and that she could not afford to be around when he did. If going to Wichita meant an opportunity to latch onto a new meal ticket, then it made sense to go.

He did not disappoint her. They checked in to the Carey House Hotel and Jake told her the story of Carrie Nation taking a hatchet to the bar and rocks to the mirror. He drove her around town to a few of the nicer shops, at one point dropping her off for an hour to spend by herself at the recently built Kress Building, telling her to buy whatever she wanted. She figured he was off taking care of whatever business he had. She made small talk with the clerk and soon realized they were in too nice of a section of town for her to find a gangster meaner and tougher than Jake.

They stayed in and ate dinner at the restaurant inside the Carey House that evening. Jake was acting more refined, like a nouveau riche businessman who was getting a chance to enjoy the finer things in life. He cut his steak in small pieces and chewed with appreciation. He sipped his wine admiringly, as though he knew anything about wine other than it was made by Dagos. He gently wiped the corners of his mouth with his napkin. For a brief moment she wasn't scared. This was the way it was supposed to be. If only he could be more like Mr. Jake Hickey rather than 'Crazy' Jake.

She stopped thinking about it. There was no *if* to consider. It wouldn't be like this permanently. She needed to get out and needed to start trying harder to do so.

Jake sat back with a self-satisfied grin on his face. Even he was enjoying the elegance he didn't realize he had been missing. He knew she was into all of this, the silk and crystal and fine China. He figured he could get used to it, too.

They went to the Orpheum and took in a movie, *Jimmy the Gent* with James Cagney and Bette Davis. It was about a con man trying to win back his girl by putting on the Ritz and acting all high-fallutin'. Silly to think a guy would have to change his basic nature to fit in and get a dame. They walked out of the theater arm in arm.

"You like all this?" She nodded, either like a young schoolgirl or an obedient puppy. "Well, there's going to be more of it." At this point, there was no reason for her to show any extreme excitement or ask any questions. She recognized when Jake had the floor. "We're doing well. I've put together a good gang and we're taking in some nice hauls. I'm putting a bankroll together. I'll be able to take over that town soon."

Heather felt her chest cave in and her stomach collapse. There was a cold fire running up and down her arms and legs. She hoped she didn't appear as pale as she felt. Jake was planning to stay in Arkansas City, planning to make a move against men who had lived there all their lives and knew the ins and outs. He was going to try to use old-fashioned Chicago muscle in a part of the country that had its own way. She knew he was going to get crushed like a mosquito on a hot summer's day. That would be just fine for her but she also couldn't run the risk of being taken down in the process.

"Why not here?" she asked, inquisitively.

He shook his head lightly. "Too big of a city. I don't have a big enough group to do it. It's taken us nearly a year to figure things out down there. They're not like us." It should have felt comforting he was including her verbally in the situation they were in. She should have been proud to be considered a partner in some small fashion. All she felt were the invisible shackles that bound her to him. At this point, it would have been better for her to keep quiet and let him go on, not make him aware of her continued displeasure. It was the sick feeling in the pit of her stomach that caused her to speak.

"Jake, why don't we just go home?"

She saw him grit his teeth and press his lips firmly together as though he were trying to prevent a violent outburst, an explosion of red-hot anger that could have taken the entire city block apart.

"Chicago is not our home any more. I go back, I get killed." He stopped suddenly, turning to her and glaring. Then his face turned from pink to red and his eyes became black. "Unless that's what you want, huh? That what you want? I've seen half a dozen little honeys in this town just today who would love the chance to hang on my arm like you're doing now." He pulled out a large bankroll and stuck a twenty-dollar bill in her ample cleavage. "See how far you go on that." It was less than the $200 he had thrown down earlier. Her value was decreasing by the minute.

"No, Jake. No." She looked down for a moment and then slowly and lovingly back up, looking directly at him, the old wanton look in her eyes. "Why don't we go back up to the hotel and I'll make it up to you."

At this point, she knew she needed to earn even the paltry $20 he was offering.

Chapter Twenty-Seven

There was a funeral in a big church, stone and marble exquisitely cut, massive stained glass windows with recreations of the Stations of the Cross, and majestic sounds from a century's old pipe organ. Altar boys in crisp clean white starched tunics and hair parted down the middle sang like eminent *castrati* a fine Requiem mass worthy of the cognoscenti of the Old World. The gown she wore was fine black silk, imported directly from Chinese merchants. Her face was a peaceful shade of cream. The mortician's skill was such that it was not possible to tell how she died.

The images melted like the remnants of snow in the Flint Hills until it became a wooden framed church in the prairie; a plain white frock and bruises on her face from the lack of effort by the country doctor in charge of the funeral parlor; little boys in overalls and plaid shirts standing barefoot and wearing straw hats; and no one save the minister and his wife playing an out of tune upright piano in the sanctuary. A raw, stark, cold wind blowing through the meager building whistled a dirge.

It really didn't matter which image came to her in her sleep. She would die a lonely death because she had bought a one-way ticket on the wrong train. Heather Devore realized she needed to double her efforts to find someone to help her escape from the disaster named

Jake Hickey. Otherwise, one of the dreams would come true.

She targeted Jimmy O'Donnell. The kid was younger than her and perhaps not as practiced at lovemaking as the boys back in the Windy City. He had the pedigree and knew his way around a gun and a gang. Whether or not he would want to go up against Jake and take him down with nothing more than promises was still yet to be seen. She sensed he could be enticed. However, there weren't many opportunities to approach him considering that Jake was constantly planning one job or another. She casually ran into him outside of Kanotex one afternoon on the pretense she was there to surprise Jake. Boldly, she questioned his decision to hang around with someone so volatile.

"This same thing happened in Chicago. George Moran—you know, Bugs—told Jake to lay off a bar in their territory. But Jake wouldn't listen. He really thought the guy was working for Capone. Now, that took a lot of smoothing over by George after Jake gave the guy a beating."

"So, why are you with him?"

"I haven't found anything better in this town. Yet."

She sashayed away toward the front entrance, wrapping her arms around Jake the moment he came out, and kissing him in a way Jimmy O'Donnell could only imagine. Another time, there was a regular meeting of Jake and the guys at Junior's. Heather made sure to lean over and kiss Jake, showing a good deal of cleavage that perhaps few of these men had seen in a while. She daringly entered the men's washroom when she knew Jimmy had gone in and found him washing his hands. She approached him as he stood there in shock and made him aware of how passionately she could kiss. Jimmy didn't have to imagine any more.

"I think I may have found something better."

She turned and slowly peeked out the door to make sure no one was coming in, bending over slightly to present her derriere in an inviting fashion. Jimmy stood there with wet hands, a throbbing erection, and a desire to have her any way he could, even if it meant crossing Jake Hickey.

Jimmy may have been the ideal target, but she wasn't willing to put all her eggs in one basket. She could see that Sean Brennan, despite his movie star looks, was capable of being as hot headed as Jake. The question was whether he would be willing to overturn the apple cart or if his pretty face was more important to him. She had learned a pleasing technique from a French courtesan who was visiting her sister in Chicago several years ago and was happy to perform it on Brennan in a back alley. The romantic nature of the act seemed to disappear on a dirt street behind a men's clothing store. For all his experience, Brennan never had a woman on her knees worshipping his manliness. This was something he could get used to. He had to consider what he would need to sacrifice to obtain it.

There was no shame in any of this. It was her looks and her body and her willingness that bought her a life of leisure and luxury that now had turned into a desperate existence. It was going to take anything and everything to get her out.

****

In spite of his exquisite wardrobe, Abram Dutcher blended in as though he were just another pebble on a beach. He had been in plain sight without anyone realizing he continued to be a fixture in Arkansas City. No one could imagine how much pull he still might have. The silent ones often can make the loudest noise.

His intention was to determine just how far along Jake Hickey had come in expanding his finances and influence. For the time being, it seemed a small group of less than ten men had the means to enjoy all the finer things Wichita, Kansas or Oklahoma City, Oklahoma had to offer. No one was well off enough to purchase the influence of politicians. In essence, they were still petty thieves with silk handkerchiefs, cock-of-the-walk attitudes, and Michigan bank rolls.

At this rate, Dutcher felt Hickey would either make enough money to leave town altogether or make a large enough mistake to get cut down like Pretty Boy Floyd just did in Ohio. That might not happen, however, as the Federal agents didn't have any interest in someone small time like Hickey.

The concerns Dutcher had were Hickey's moll, a sexy filly who was using all of her own personal weapons to stir the pot. At least two of Hickey's men had encounters with her that he was aware of. This was the powder keg that Witherspoon spoke of, the fuse placed there by a dangerous woman.

Heather was in the lingerie section of Harrison's Ladies Clothing Store when the elderly Dutcher sidled up alongside. Her eyes glistened and her mouth was moist as she felt the lovely silk undergarments, imagining them next to her body.

"Lovely, aren't they?" A brief gasp escaped her as her spell was broken. "My apologies. I did not mean to startle you." She looked around. There was no one else in their vicinity.

"I haven't seen stuff like this in a long time."

"I do not believe women often consider their own desires enough."

"I know what I like." Her smile was not aimed at the old guy. It was more of a reflection of own thoughts.

"Knowing what you like is important. Achieving it is an altogether different matter. And too many times, we are disappointed with the results."

He tipped his hat, smiled and walked away. She went back to admiring the lingerie, wondering who she was going to get to buy it for her.

****

Hallett sat in Childers' chair behind the big desk. He imagined himself a senator in Washington, D.C. with a staff the size of a small farming community but dressed in finely tailored business suits with polished shoes so shiny you could shave in them. A crystal decanter would be on his desk, knowing that the seat of the government would be different than the entire backward state of Kansas that still refused to acknowledge the law of the land. He would be on committees and be a confidant to the President and respected for his fairness and no-nonsense attitude. None of these dreams would come true with a fly buzzing around, that being Jake Hickey.

"You're letting this punk get out of control."

Childers, for his part, was projecting a dominant and controlled appearance, standing upright with his chest puffed out and his nostrils flared, eyes wide and gazing straight ahead. Inside, he knew Hallett's connections could cause his refinery to go under, or something worse.

"These guys are not doing anything locally. They're not drawing attention to us. I don't see where there's a problem."

Hallett's fist smashed down on the desk. Childers jumped, nearly bringing both feet of the ground. There was now a small dry lump in his throat.

"The local market has dried up, Martin. With repeal, booze is legal. This town doesn't have the traffic to support the girls you run into and out of that piss-hole of a hotel. These guys are doing what we should be doing."

"Maybe, we can..." Childers didn't have any viable ideas but at least wanted to sound like he did. Hallett knew this puppet was losing his strings.

"What? Maybe we can what? This guy, this Hickey needs to be gone."

"You want me to send some cars to The Gladstone and blast him as he steps out? This isn't Cicero."

"We send him away, just like Capone."

"How?"

Hallett stood there, fingertips of each hand lightly pressing the desk, like Horowitz contemplating a piece by Rachmaninoff.

"That broad of his. She's stirring things up. Have you heard?"

"I've heard." Childers knew where this was going but it made no sense to argue.

****

Jake decided not to go to work that day. He was getting close to never going back to his so-called job at the refinery. He was ready to move forward. It might have to be without Heather. She was growing cold and distant, not giving in to him when he wanted her which

161

made him want her less and caused him to think of whether she was really needed. Instead of just dumping her in town, it was better for him to give her a stake and let her go where she wanted as long as it was countless miles from where he was. It occurred to him it might be better if she was far enough away to forget.

All this time here had not softened his dislike for the small Kansas town. He did, however, recognize the opportunities that were being presented. He was no second fiddle to a bigwig. Despite the presence of a few businessmen and politicos who had dirty hands, this was nothing like the syndicate in Chicago. Back there, he was a button man, a gunsel, a soldier. Here, he was his own boss. It finally dawned on him that as long as he stuck with Bugs Moran, he would never get the chance to run his own outfit. George was no different than Hallett or Childers in that regard. Being sent down here was a blessing in disguise. It may have been a smaller pond but he certainly was the big fish.

Whatever this diner called the sandwich, it wasn't corned beef. Why the heck were they serving it on white bread? Probably had no idea what rye bread was. Even with a thick slab of mustard it was barely edible. The food was something that would take a long time to get used to, especially if he were making moves to take over. His throat was tighter than the small booth.

From out of nowhere Officer Witherspoon slid in to the seat opposite. His blank look was neither warm nor threatening. It was even less appetizing than the so-called corned beef sandwich.

"Something I can do for you, officer?" Jake's annoyance was clear.

"What was it like growing up?"

Hickey shook his head like it had been stung by a bee. "What?"

"Growing up. What was your childhood like?"

Jake placed his sandwich on the plate and casually wiped the crumbs from his fingers. When put on the spot, he felt a need to keep his hands free. "I had to fend for myself. Everything I got, I got for myself. It wasn't much, but it was mine." His attempts at being stoic and proud only wound up sounding bitter and aloof. "What about you?"

Baron leaned forward, looking like a naughty little child who was about to confess breaking his mother's vase. "You know, I honestly don't remember. But I realize it doesn't matter. My youth, the war, none of it. Because, Mr. Hale, I'm here today. Not a punk kid who thought he could fit in if he hung around a bunch of bad boys. Not a hotshot who threw away a chance at a good life because his buddies were more important. Me. I'm here. Right now." Hickey stared directly at Baron, not allowing his face to move or twitch, not letting a frown or smile even consider alighting. "I knew a kid who was tougher and angrier than I was. Never negotiated. Never met anyone halfway. He was a vicious monster. But he became something important. I guess if you call being a gangster important. I got out because I knew the only road led to death. If I was going to die, I wanted it to be meaningful. But I lived. And I figured I could do some good." Baron started laughing which caught Hickey off guard. He couldn't tell if the policeman was starting to go crazy. It was understandable living in a town like this. "What do you suppose that kid from back in the day would say if he saw me now?"

It was Hickey's turn to lean in. Baron didn't back

away. Hickey's eyes were black as coal, his nostrils flaring with flames ready to project.

"He'd probably say you were a sucker for thinking you could do a damn bit of good in this burg."

Baron smiled. "I think you're wrong, Mr. Hale. I don't think he'd say anything."

"Why is that?"

"Because he's probably dead."

Jake knew right then it was Eric Kimble sitting in front of him. The scars and the pieces of flesh covered what he remembered but the eyes gave him away. It wasn't going to be Madison and State Street like Two-Gun Alterie recommended. It would be Summit Avenue in Arkansas City, Kansas.

Jake wiped his mouth of the excess mustard, stood up, and left a dollar bill and some coins on the table. "I wouldn't recommend the corned beef."

Hickey walked out. He certainly wasn't concerned about Childers or Hallett or Heather Devore. He wouldn't have been afraid of a Kansas lawman named Baron Witherspoon. A tough kid from his old neighborhood with a badge gave him pause for thought. This town was not going to hold them both for long.

Chapter Twenty-Eight

I made a mistake, and I knew it. I allowed myself to be that hotheaded Irish kid from the neighborhood, the scrappy one who spoke before he thought, and always felt a gun was the answer to most problems. I had spent sixteen years struggling to become Baron Witherspoon, not just in name, but the way he was to me, my buddy, my friend, my comrade in arms. The guy who looked at someone and determined they could use a hand regardless of their background. I bet he would have treated me the same way if, for some reason, I met him right here in Ark City rather than in the war. That was who I was trying to become. In one brief moment, I let a thug and a second-rate gangster drag me down to his level. That would have only meant other people getting injured or killed. It was necessary to do everything possible to just keep this between him and me.

His girl was struggling to find anyone to help. This wasn't Chicago or New York or even Wichita. This was a place of farmers and refinery workers and mill men and a few bad men who were getting too tired to fight back. This was a town where people had one good suit they wore on Sunday and who might get fancy and out of line at a barn dance. I knew about places like Junior's and rooms set aside in The Gladstone where Phil Garmes directed men of leisure and money. This town was not Sodom and Gomorrah but the Pope wasn't planning on visiting any time soon either.

There was no sense on going back to talk with Childers. He was a sly worm who was also too scared to do anything wrong and wind up bringing everything crashing down around him. Councilman Hallett was not going to give me the time of day either, especially considering the way he brushed aside that shooting investigation and me in the process. If there was an easier solution to Hickey, he was going to find it and it sure wasn't going to have anything to do with the police. So, I visited with Chief Taylor in his office. He spoke like he was walking on eggshells. Then again, so was I.

"I'm of the belief," I said, "that Jack Hale is actually Jake Hickey from Chicago. He's known as *Crazy* Jake and was a lieutenant to Bugs Moran."

"Why would he be here?"

"It's my opinion that many Chicago gangsters have been here in the past and probably several are here now. When the heat is on, they need a place to stay out of sight. I guess you might call this Little Chicago."

"That's only speculation, Officer Witherspoon."

"Well, the part about Hickey is accurate."

"How do you know?"

Despite the fact that Chief Taylor directed me toward Abram Dutcher, he had been distant of late. I was never able to be sure if he was on the dole or just being extremely cautious. I respected him but had to make sure I could trust him. "For now, let's just say I have reliable sources."

Chief Taylor seemed on the verge of a confession the likes of which would have made a priest proud. His face contorted and then straightened out again. He took on the look of a teacher, a man with the knowledge but not the ability. He cleared his throat like a pastor about to start an important sermon. "Back in '25, Chief Floyd Higgins was informed by Mayor Boggs that he was to be in complete charge of the police department. He was given the authority to make any decisions he chose. One of the first was to release three employees: Charles Lee, William Lemmon, and Emma Ray. You see, Chief Higgins tried to do this before but his actions were blocked by previous mayors. You have to understand, Officer Witherspoon, without that kind of support, we might as well just go back to the Anti Horse Thief Association."

He came around to the front of the desk, sat on the edge, and leaned as close to my ear as possible. His words were meant for me and me alone.

"I can not go into detail but my hands are tied on this. This Hale or Hickey is either going to take over or be a stain in the road."

"I understand, sir."

"I don't think you do, son. If other people are not able to take him out of the picture, he cannot be allowed to run things. There's a kind of, well, balance here. Ark City can bear only so much before it cracks. You ever hear of Iowa City? Also called Iowa Point."

"I don't believe so."

"Up in Doniphan County not far from St. Joe. They had a couple of guys with a notion to steal business from the Missouri side. Already struggling from the Civil War. Before that, businessmen were taking in $1000 a day. Well, their post office just closed down last year. Hardly any residents any more. Before long, no one will remember them."

It seems like he was telling me to take care of the situation no matter what otherwise Jake Hickey could burn this town to the ground. I knew what I could do. I still didn't know how I would fare in the end. Maybe that was just it. Maybe it wasn't my say in the matter. As much as I tried to honor and respect the memory of a good friend, my time may have been at hand.

I was walking through the station house just after speaking with the chief when Dr. Brenz came upon me. His look reminded me of my own father when I'd get out of line.

"Officer Witherspoon, you are overdue for your examination."

"I'll have to catch up with you later, Doctie. Got a lot going at the moment."

"Now." His voice echoed. A few officers stopped their chatting and looked in the general direction. I nodded and followed him dutifully like there was starch in my shorts.

At his office, he ran through the usual steps: heart, blood pressure, reflexes. Then he examined my facial scars more closely than he had ever done before. I knew he had read up on it when I came back from the war, trying to help however he could. He admitted he was no expert on the subject but was able to give me some advice here and there whenever there was some discomfort. It wasn't like he was going to change fields at this stage of his life.

"Been reading about a doctor named McIndoe. New Zealand, I think. Related to that Dr. Gillies who performed all those surgeries during the war. This McIndoe's just been given a Fellowship of the

American College of Surgeons."

"And?"

"There's talk of new surgical procedures. They might be able to reduce more of the scarring, perhaps make you look more like yourself."

I wasn't sure what he was getting at. For the first several years after the war, my physical wellbeing was all he was concerned about. It was only the past five years or so that he had been helping me with the dreams and the dark cloud hanging over me on occasion. Every effort he had been previously making was to encourage me to have as normal a life as possible. Now he was suggesting something to make me look more like Baron Witherspoon.

"You know who I am, Doctie?" I asked, boldly.

"I believe so."

"The people in town, you think they know who I am?"

"Certainly."

"Then there's really no need to make me look like something."

"Not like something, Baron. Like you."

I still couldn't tell if this was one of his notions to help me keep my head on straight or if he had something else brewing. Like a North wind, a notion blew into my mind.

"What truly makes a man who he is? You see, I think it's what he does and how he acts. Not how he looks. That's the real man. And I've done everything I could for the past sixteen years to show people who I really am. I don't have to remind you what the war did to me, how it took me and chewed me up and spat me out. Took a lot of people to get me right, especially you."

For a moment, I wondered how Baron Witherspoon would have dealt with Jake Hickey and then I realized he would be no match for him. He was too good of a kid to be hard-nosed and tough. Probably would have come back from the war and worked on his dad's farm or got himself a good paying job at a factory or refinery. He wouldn't have worked as a police officer, even as much of a hero as he was. The irony was I could do a better job as a police officer than he could.

"Right now, though, it's not how I look that's gonna matter. It's what I do. I can't tell you much, but if I don't act the way I need to, a whole lot of people are going to get hurt."

He put his hand on my shoulder, the way Baron's dad would have.

"This town needs you, Baron."

I put on my undershirt and then my uniform, looking down at the badge pinned to it. People often talk about who you were or who you are now. Some think about who they might become. In order to face down Jake Hickey, I'd have to be a little bit Baron Witherspoon and a lot of Eric Kimble.

It was when I went back to the station I learned the stakes had just gotten higher.

Chapter Twenty-Nine

It was Phil Garmes that called it in to the station. I never heard why he had gone up to the room. Knowing Phil, it was something shady but he'd probably stick to the "bringing up fresh towels" story to make himself sound like a good employee to his bosses, maybe even keep his job.

The desk sergeant turned me right around when I was finished with my check-up, told me to hightail it over to The Gladstone. I found Big Ray Vernon in the lobby, shaking his head, and wiping his forehead with a handkerchief. His eyes were glazed over, as though he'd seen a seven-foot rabbit, or something equally confounding. He had the shakes like a fever patient or lunatic.

"It's awful, Baron. Just awful. There's all...There's all that blood. Blood everywhere. There's just so much blood. They're never gonna clean it all up. It's awful." His voice was hoarse and cracking, mouth so dry and lips parched. The scene had drained the life out of him. I reached up and grabbed him by the shoulders, trying to snap him out of the deep hole he had fallen into.

"What is it, Ray?"

"The woman. He cut her throat."

This kid hadn't seen anything truly horrible that life was capable of creating. I prayed he never would be in the position I was in all those years ago. Right now, he wasn't doing me a darn bit of good. I gently leaned him back against the wall then raced up the stairs where one officer was standing outside the door while Dave Morton was questioning Phil Garmes.

"I was bringing up fresh towels. They seemed to use a lot of towels. The door was open. I pushed it wider and I saw—" Phil didn't break apart like Big Ray but he just stopped. Completely frozen. Unable to continue. All of his petty dealings weren't able to prepare him for this. It was like seeing the light at a tent revival.

Two other officers were in the room, looking over every detail and taking minor notes. They recognized me as I stepped into the room. Heather Devore was laying on the floor curled up in a ball, bra and panties her only clothing, lying in a pool of blood that had come from her neck. A bloody straight razor had been dropped by her head. Big Ray was right. They never would be able to clean it all up.

I went back outside stepping squarely in front of Phil, talking so loud the wind of my breath nearly knocked him over. I was hoping my sheer volume would end up causing a ringing in his ears.

"Where is he?"

"Who?" he said, blankly.

"Hickey. The guy who's lived here for over a year."

"I don't know."

I grabbed his shirt and pulled him close to me.

"I don't know," he yelped louder. At this point, he looked like a stray dog that had nowhere else to go.

"I bet if I contact Chicago they'll advise me about several warrants out on him. That means you've been harboring a fugitive in our town. Your penny ante bunk means nothing compared to that, Phillie. We'll send you far away to do hard time with a lot of bad men. They don't cotton to little worms like you."

"I haven't seen him since last night. They had supper in the room and then he left." He was shouting just as loud, fear taking over his entire body.

"Where did he go?" I yanked him closer, gripping the shirt tighter.

"I don't know."

I let go of him forcefully, practically throwing him from my grip and not caring much where he landed. "Let's go," I said to Dave.

"Where?"

"Kanotex."

"What about him?"

I looked back at him, finally able to say what I had wanted to for so long. "He's good for nothing."

The sad thing was I didn't have time to consider the abrupt and violent end that Heather Devore met. I'd met a few gals of her type during the war. I knew what they were after and I didn't mind or judge. The worst that would have happened was they got old and lost their appeal. They might settle down with a rich old man who thought they looked just fine. But not this. For all her faults, especially hooking up with someone like Jake Hickey, she certainly didn't deserve this. Sometimes, deserve has got nothing to do with it.

We grabbed Big Ray on the way out and practically marched over to Kanotex. By that time, Ray was looking for a way out of his doldrums. He needed to do something to try and shake the image of that bloody scene out of his head. With me prepared to talk tall and loud, I might just have been his cure.

The three of us walked into the main office of Kanotex and right past the secretary whose feeble efforts to stop us fell on deaf ears. Martin Childers sat behind his big desk talking on his phone. He hung up as soon as we walked in. I made sure he knew how serious I was by slamming my hands on the desk.

"Jake Hickey. Where is he?"

"Who?"

"Maybe you know him as Jack Hale."

"Officer, you're going to have to…"

"Short. Greasy hair. Bad attitude. A smile you want to slap off his face."

"What's this about?"

I lowered my voice. Instead of volume, I recognized a sinister bitterness. I just wasn't willing to let him control the situation any more. "His girl's been murdered."

Childers feigned deep concern in the same way a man tells a bawdy joke. "That's awful." His emotion changed just as quickly as he spoke into the Flexifone. "Ms. Prentiss, please locate Jack Hale's foreman and send him to my office." The next few minutes felt like walking through a minefield. No one spoke. No one hardly moved. There really wasn't anything to do or say. Childers had lost some of his bravado but it was still his office and his refinery. It was like being in the enemy's trenches. Unless he made a move, you could do nothing. I could see the scene play out in my head when the foreman finally did arrive. *We were just dotting the Is and crossing the Ts.* Either Childers was protecting Hickey or was throwing him to the wolves. Either way, this was a waste of our time. At least, I would be laying my cards on the table.

Sure enough, when the foreman came in, he indicated he hadn't seen Jack Hale in several days and was preparing paperwork to formally recommend firing him. Such was the upstanding nature of this man he was unable to accept a worker not following his orders. The smile on Childers face was far too satisfied, as though he had done everything that was expected of him and was in the clear. I knew my goal was Jake Hickey but I hadn't forgotten who ran things in this town. I made sure to let him know.

"I'm not through with you Childers. Not by a long shot."

"You have no idea who you're dealing with."

"Yes, I do. I think you folks are the ones in the dark." I turned and left, followed by my two comrades. We headed back to the station where I instructed Ray and Dave to grab shotguns. George McAllister had come on duty and I filled him in with all the necessary details. I went to Chief Taylor's office to advise him where we stood. I also told him I'd be needing the tommy-gun. We all remembered about a year ago, September of '33, when Vice Chief Robinson headed down to the Missouri Pacific rail yards to, well, interrogate a bunch of hoboes after the Drive-In Market holdup. After a demonstration of the tommy-gun on an old wash boiler, they were gone the next morning. At that time, Robinson quoted something by President Teddy Roosevelt about carrying a big stick. I figured the tommy-gun made a suitable substitute.

I talked to the guys, advising them what we needed to do. Locating Jake Hickey and bringing him in was the most important thing. We weren't looking to shoot him on sight. There was still a possibility of making a deal with him and bringing down the whole paper tower. I knew things had been stable and quiet before he came along. If I had to make a sacrifice it would have been leaving Childers and whoever else in charge and taking Hickey out of the picture.

There was a tiny mosquito buzzing in my ear, trying to make me think where I didn't want to, forcing me to come to terms with my own emotions. Was I trying to eliminate Hickey so I could stay as I was without admitting anything? Could what I had done been considered so outside the law the county might actually want to prosecute me? I thought about Jake Hickey more and more. As a young man, he was wild and impulsive, capable of harming anyone or anything. It seems like he had only gotten worse as he grew up. So, I wound up convincing myself that taking out Jake Hickey was the best thing for Ark City. It just so happened it was the best thing for me as well.

Then I realized the most important thing was for me to stay alive. If Jake somehow came out on top, he would tarnish the legacy of Baron Witherspoon, the legacy I was building for my dead friend. I, Eric Kimble, didn't matter anymore. I had died a long time ago.

Chapter Thirty

Jake hadn't gone to his so-called job for a while. It didn't seem necessary. Back when Bugs Moran sent him out of Chicago fearing repercussions after Capone was sent to prison, he knew he had to keep a low profile. As much as he hated the backwoods town, he realized it was best for him to come to this out of the way corner of Kansas to avoid the law or other gangs. But time had made him grow weary, and his patience wore out. The need to get back into the action meant he was no longer going to stay quiet.

Hallett and Childers hardly ever used the tunnels anymore. Jake had a notion to open a bawdy house in some of the rooms, after they'd been cleaned up a bit, of course. Give it a little class and show the hicks how things were done, Chicago-style. He could run a little empire underneath the streets of Arkansas City, Kansas and leave the top side to the bigwigs and politicos. It was almost like dividing a twenty-four hour period into day and night. That would have made things fair if Jake had any concept of the notion.

He and Dietrich were using one of the rooms to store stolen loot from various jobs around the area. They kept their noses clean while in town. As far as he was concerned, he was simply going out on his own and trying not to step on anyone's toes. He wasn't sure how these business relationships worked in these parts and he didn't want to start a war, especially if he didn't have enough allies to support him.

Sean Brennan sprinted from the north end of the Summit Ave. tunnel. His dapper appearance seemed somewhat ruffled.

"There's four cops patrolling the street."

"So?" Jake didn't give it too much thought, even with Brennan's breathless commentary.

"It looks like something bad. They're on the prowl for something."

Jake put the clipboard with the inventory on one of the cartons and nodded to Dietrich. "Let's blow. We'll pick this up later after we've figured out what's going on."

They started walking toward the south end.

"What are you doing? They're down at that end, near the flower shop. That's why I came in through the hardware store."

Jake was growing annoyed with Brennan. He was the type to always make a snide comment but then back off, acting as though he never meant anything he said. He did have a vicious streak that could come out like a rattlesnake. Jake saw that in Texas when he slammed a bank's security guard in the head with his gun just because he didn't like guards or cops. Now, however, he was showing fear of the police and that was something Jake wouldn't abide.

He and Dietrich continued toward the flower shop entrance and were about fifty feet from the steps leading up when Jake, patting his jacket pockets, realized he had left the Browning back in the storage room. He told Dietrich to continue on, take a careful look out on the street and be prepared to advise him what he saw. He had just grabbed his automatic off the pile of boxes and was walking back toward the south when he heard a single gunshot followed by a blast from a tommy-gun. He ran back toward the north end when he came upon Brennan who decided he wasn't going to take any chances. They ran together toward the north and the exit by the hardware store.

Brennan pushed Jake back when they got to the stairs, peeking up the steps, turning his head to catch any sounds. He took two steps, stopped, and looked back to Jake. They took a step at a time with Jake always two steps back. The second step from the top squeaked loudly, catching Brennan off guard and causing him to freeze in his tracks. No lights were shining through the windows of the hardware store, which was closed. One of their guys, a kid from St. Louis, was working there when not pulling jobs and had got them a key to the place after discovering the other entrance. It made it easier for them to come and go as they needed.

When they were both in the store, they closed and locked the door to the tunnel and carefully went to the front door. They could see lantern lights toward the south end of the street. They shined in a cluster amid muffled sounds of heated discussions. They could only assume Dietrich was caught or killed. Brennan grabbed Jake by the lapel and pulled him toward the back door.

This was what Jake feared most: getting pinned down in a city with no hideouts and very few friends other than his gang. Only two contingency plans remained: drive up north to their guns and ammo man who had a farm or Junior's where the proprietor was friendly to their cause, especially after a $1000 donation. Jake figured if the cops were finally on to him, finally ready to bring it to a showdown, then Junior's might be the first place they'd look, especially since the policeman who called himself Baron Witherspoon knew he frequented the place. The thing to do now was get to one of their cars and head out. He'd either have to come back for Heather or leave her. His neck was in the noose now.

They were easily five blocks from the railroad tracks where they parked one of the vehicles on the south end of town. They would have to cross the street somehow and sneak down behind buildings to Adams Ave., circling around the cluster of cops, and then cut across to the tracks. At that point, the easiest thing to do was head south out of town despite the fact their friend lived north. The last thing Jake wanted was a shootout. Not yet. They had caught him off guard. He wondered whether Childers had anything to do with this. The guys who supposedly ran things were weak and would turn to small time antics like ratting on one of their own. Back in Chicago, it was direct and complete, like the way Capone took care of Frankie Yale and Joe Aiello. Sure, you needed cops and politicos on the take to leave you alone but you took care of business for yourself. When he had cleared out and collected himself, he would figure who ratted him out.

Apparently, no attention was being paid to the southeast end of town, just on the other side of Summit Ave. To be cautious, they continued down and crossed at Jefferson. With fewer businesses, mostly small houses or random buildings, and no lights on them, it was easier to make their way east toward the railroad tracks.

Jake and Sean began weaving in and out of buildings, often getting separated by a hundred feet or so. At one point, Jake lost track of Brennan but figured he knew where they were heading and continued moving fast, ducking low, and keeping the Browning at the ready.

It was less than a block to go to get to the car. Jake could make out the car through the trees. While running, he looked quickly back to see if he could locate Brennan. It was too dark. As he turned back, Officer Witherspoon was standing in his path not fifty feet away. He stopped suddenly.

"I'm told this thing fires 800 shots a minute. That means it's a lot faster than you." Officer Witherspoon had an unhealthy smile on his face as though he were enjoying this situation more than he should be. That annoyed Jake.

Hickey raised his hands and dropped his gun. There was no need to worry at this point. He figured it was a gun charge. The Ark City cops had nothing on him regarding any of the jobs they had pulled. He hadn't considered that Dietrich was coming out of the flower shop and could only hope he had locked and hidden the door to the tunnel.

"You'll get no trouble from me, copper." The cockiness of *Crazy* Jake was in full bloom.

Baron motioned with the barrel of the tommy-gun. "On your knees." Jake cooperated. Baron approached with slow measured steps, holding the tommy-gun firm while taking out his handcuffs. Preparing for potential resistance, he used quick and firm force to affix the shackles before he jerked Hickey up to his feet, placing the end of the barrel to Jake's nose.

"They pay you to grab me?" This is how Jake imagined the big payout, the end, his death. He figured it would go bloody and in the dark.

"You have any idea why I'm arresting you, Mr. Hale?" Using Jake's fake name and stressing it sharply was Baron's way of letting him know the game was up.

"I was carrying that gun, officer. What kind of time you get in this state for that?"

Baron lowered the barrel of the tommy-gun and stood directly in front of Hickey's face.

"Your woman, Ms. Devore, is dead."

Jake went pale and cold. His eyes stared straight but he didn't see Baron two inches from him.

"Had her throat slit by your straight razor. Now, why'd you go and do that?"

The slight shake in Jake's head built like an earthquake, making him look like he had epilepsy. "No. No. You got it all wrong. I didn't do that. I had no reason to."

"You know what? I figured that might be the case. But the way it looks, you're gonna take the fall."

Baron grabbed Jake's arm roughly, pulling it tight and straining his hands in back of him. Jake tried pulling away but Baron grabbed him even tighter.

"This is wrong and you know it." Hickey's pleas fell on deaf ears. There was a long walk back before the other officers were going to catch up and help bring him to the jail. He figured he had a small chance to make this copper listen, even if it did sound like a lot of big crazy talk. He knew there was no way to make a deal but he'd have to try.

Chapter Thirty-One

On one of my previous patrols, I had come across an unregistered car over by the rail tracks between Jefferson and Madison. I made note of it for future reference but let it be. Might have been someone from a small farm who came into town for some fun and got a might too unstable to drive. It was nothing to focus on. At the time.

After discovering Heather Devore and meeting with Childers, I had an unsettling feeling. It just didn't seem like the kind of thing a gangster from Chicago would do. Nothing could be gained from it. If she were talking too much or threatening his business, she probably would have been taken somewhere and dumped. We might not have Lake Michigan but there are plenty of sunflower fields and lakes around. This seemed like so much more, like everything was pointing directly to Hickey, as though someone wanted us to pay attention to him and only him. At this point, it was working.

Big Ray, Dave Morton, George McAllister and I started combing as much of the city as possible. We heard a minor commotion in a flower shop on North Summit, almost like a knocking over of boxes at an hour when no one should have been there. A tall man in a dark suit was roaming around. We shined our lanterns on him, yelling for him to come out. He stood near the door and fired on us. I unleashed the power of the tommy-gun on him, and he fell. Perhaps I had let the emotions of dealing with Childers get the better of me but I certainly was not going to allow anyone to shoot at us.

None of us recognized him. His face was a statue etched in stone. The cheekbones, forehead, and jaw all looked like they could put a dent in the hood of a car. He had no identification anywhere on his person. Whoever he was, he died probably the same as he lived.

The four of us used a two person weave pattern throughout the rest of the town. The dead guy was not the killer of Ms. Devore and we still had Hickey to find if for no other reason than he was the prime suspect. I got separated from Big Ray just past Central. It was north of Adams I heard the sounds of men's shoes on pavement. My guess was two guys and possibly two options: south out of town to an open area or east toward the rail tracks. I remembered the car and headed east.

I stood just behind a tree within sight of the car as a single pair of shoes came clicking rapidly in my direction. The man slowed, turned, and then stood facing me in the dark. It was Jake Hickey.

"I'm told this thing fires 800 shots a minute. That means it's a lot faster than you." All the playing around and cheap banter was over. I had him right before me. I was prepared and able to take him down if that's what it took but I preferred to turn him into a canary if I could.

"You'll get no trouble from me, copper." He raised his hands and looked at me with a smile as though I just caught him jaywalking.

I approached him slowly, keeping the gun leveled

at his gut. I slid around in back of him, keeping the finger of one hand on the trigger while my other hand reached on my belt for handcuffs. This would be a tricky move without another officer present so I decided to work quick and hard. I jerked one of his hands swiftly behind him, placed one end of the cuff on, then using the hand holding the gun grabbed his other hand and cuffed it as well. I didn't mind the pain I was inflicting on him. I jerked him to his feet and turned him to face me.

"They pay you to grab me?" He still didn't realize this wasn't Chicago.

"You have any idea why I'm arresting you, Mr. Hale?" He knew I knew who he was. We both knew each other.

"I was carrying that gun, officer. What kind of time you get in this state for that?"

Any gangster would have played deaf and dumb, so I figured this for a response. I needed to make sure that my ideas of what really happened had any truth to them. "Your woman, Ms. Devore, is dead. Had her throat slit by your straight razor. Now, why'd you go and do that?"

His eyes looked like a deer before you shot it. A light bead of sweat started to form on his forehead. His head was shaking. He wasn't the tough guy now, knew he couldn't joke his way out of a bad situation. And I knew that, despite the other crimes he committed, this one wasn't his.

"No. No. You got it all wrong. I didn't do that. I had no reason to."

"You know what? I figured that might be the case. But the way it looks, you're gonna take the fall."

"This is wrong and you know it."

"I'll let a judge decide that."

I started pulling him back toward Summit Ave. where I knew I'd catch up with one of the guys. It was time to put Jack Hale and Jake Hickey in a box.

"What do you need? Childers? You want to bring him down, right?"

We stopped and I turned him sharply toward me.

"You've got nothing, Hickey. You never got any orders from Childers or anyone higher up. When you were sent down here, you were told to play cool. Take a job. Live quietly. What's the matter? This kind of living ain't good enough for you?"

"I'll talk."

"And say what?"

The constant licking of his lips made me aware of the tightening he was feeling in his neck. A guy like this can only shoot his way out of a situation, not talk it out. He looked down, seeking the answer at his shoes, before looking back up at me.

"I'll tell 'em who you are."

I figured he was going to pull that rabbit out of the hat.

"Oh. And who am I, Jake?"

"You're Eric Kimble, a punk Mick gangster from Lincoln Park on the North Side of Chicago."

"I think most people around here will tell you I'm Baron Witherspoon from Arkansas City, Kansas. They'll say I've been one of the best police officers they've ever had in spite of these awful war wounds. I even know a few older ladies who think it's a shame I never got married on account of my face because it's what's in your heart that counts. What's in your heart,

Jake?"

"You bastard."

I brought the tommy-gun up to his face, sticking the barrel against his forehead. In that moment, I was Eric Kimble. It was 1916 and I was a young man with a life of criminal gang activity in my future, even though I knew it might be a short future. The payoff was big and worthwhile for a kid with nothing to lose except for his life. Guys like Hickey were either your friend or your enemy. There was no middle ground. Even if he was part of your gang, you always had to watch your back with the way he could just go off. Reminded me of The Schemer. So, we grew up in the same neighborhood. So, we were both sluggers for the Market Street Gang. It didn't matter. Hickey was *Crazy* Jake long before he got the nickname. You couldn't trust him as far as you could spit. If this was Chicago Ave. and North State Street, there would be a bullet hole in the middle of Jake Hickey's forehead right now. But then I remembered who I was and what I really needed to do. I lowered the gun.

"I'm taking you in, Hickey. We're going to investigate the murder of Heather Devore. We'll take your statement. If there is anything to it, you might get off on the murder charge."

We started walking again. It was a cool evening but I felt strangely warmed.

"What made you change?" I barely heard him. It was as though he wasn't sure if he wanted to ask.

"You wouldn't understand."

"Try me."

"You haven't seen the kind of death I've seen. What you boys in the mobs in Chicago do is nothing compared to what countries can do to each other. I understand the North Siders. I understand Bugs. It's all about the money, right? But war, that's something else. Killing that way just doesn't make any sense." I had said everything but I felt like I had said nothing. "You wouldn't understand."

"Killing always makes sense. That's what you never understood."

Maybe he was right.

Chapter Thirty-Two

I was sure proud of myself, perhaps more so than I should have been. I had this punk in my hands, finally had the upper hand on him after all these years. I can't honestly say it was any kind of payback because there wasn't any thing, any incident between him and me from our days as kids. It was just because I was on the side of the law and had him that made me happy.

On the other hand, as a policeman, I knew I was on shaky ground. Heather Devore was killed in his hotel room using his straight razor. He probably wouldn't have a decent alibi but it was all flimsy evidence. I felt fairly certain a jury would convict him if for nothing else than being a northerner. This was only a local crime, not in the jurisdiction of the Feds. We weren't going to try him on robbery charges or even income tax evasion like Capone.

What I figured had happened was Hallett and Childers had set him up. Neither Hickey nor I had any proof of this, and he knew it. He also realized he had very little to trade for his pathetic life. But I was willing to listen to him. It was ironic to be putting him away from something he didn't do to make up for all the bad things already accounted for in his ledger.

I met up with the others and we carefully escorted Hickey back to the station. I locked him in a cell that had a single bunk bed and a small sink. I hated to admit it but I liked seeing him like this. A crazy rat stuck in a cage.

"Where were you today?"

"I was—"

"Don't say at work. Childers and your foreman have already said you weren't there. Pretty much indicated you hadn't been there for a while."

His face went blank. No sadness or anger or bitterness. Just blank like he wasn't even human.

"Hallett's not coming down here to bail you out either. Seems like you've got no one looking out for you, Jake. So, where were you? You tell me, it might get you out of a jam."

"You got nothing on me."

"Your room. Your razor. Your woman. We can get fingerprints off the razor. Just like what Purvis did to catch Dillinger. Oh yeah, I read all about that. Scientific methods and all kinds of stuff. See, we ain't as backwoods as you think we are."

"No jury will convict me."

I leaned forward, my face inches from the bar, speaking low and deep and guttural. "You don't get it, Hickey. This ain't Chicago. You can't buy a jury here. You don't have that kind of muscle or dough. When twelve churchgoing, God-fearing men find out about you, they're going to send you away for a long time. You're lucky we don't have the death penalty here."

He turned away from me, walked slowly to the bunk, and sat staring at the opposite wall. He was digging in for a long fight. I figured we were done for now. As I started to walk away, he spoke quietly, like a man possessed. "They will find out about you, and they won't like it."

I turned back, looked in his direction, waited long enough for him to look at me. "I'll take my chances. What about you?"

Someone had called Chief Taylor, who was waiting for me when I came out of the jail area. He was nodding in approval but his eyes were squinting in uncertainty. "You got something that will stick?"

"Well, he can go down for this or admit to what he was really doing. In either case, he's going away."

He continued nodding. He was thinking of all the possibilities as well as not letting this fish get away. "You're going to have to take him up to Winfield."

It was the county seat. They had a bigger jail and the courthouse. Our jail usually held guys who had gotten drunk and beat up their wives or girlfriends. We didn't usually get such honored guests.

"I know. We just need to get all the evidence figured out and make sure the district attorney has everything he needs to lock this monkey up."

Chief Taylor leaned in closer, trying not to let anyone else hear. "Can we get anything out of him? You know, bring the whole thing down?"

"I'm all for fighting one battle at a time, Chief."

He nodded again. The thing that was on his mind, whatever was eating at him and causing him to worry and back off, was still there, like a bad fever that gave him the chills and wouldn't go away.

I met with my guys to impress on them the importance of this arrest. "This guy is a gangster from Chicago. Pretty big in his day but his day has passed. That doesn't mean he doesn't have a rattle no more. I'm pretty sure he's been behind all those robberies we've been reading about in the reports last several months.

Which means there is a gang out there. Three, four, five guys, maybe more. That dead guy in the flower shop for sure. I want him watched round the clock. Right now, you're the only guys I trust. We take six-hour shifts until we're ready to move him to Winfield. George, you just came on duty the latest. You take the first shift. Ray, you're next, then Dave, then me. Don't talk to him. Don't say nothing to him. If he talks, just remember what he says and write it down in a report later. Any questions?"

"You think his gang'll try to bust him out?" Ray asked.

"Can't say for sure. I figure there's one of two things that'll happen. They could pack up with their loot and take off, which would be fine by us."

"Or else?" Ray continued, apprehensively.

"They might come back looking for revenge."

"Against you?" Dave was just starting to figure out that Hickey's biggest thorn was me.

"Yeah. And anyone else in the way."

I went back to my room and tried to sleep. Took a swig from my bottle of *medicine* but that only wound me up. For the first time in a long while, the dreams were coming back. Only they weren't from the war. They went back further to city tenements and dirty streets, rats running around, men with hats and suits who didn't care about anything and looked like they bathed in twenty dollar bills. I was a scared kid looking for a better life but some kids wanted more. Kids like Jake Hickey. His dad went from meat packing to running errands to breaking arms. Whereas Jake respected his father, he knew he could do even better. I liked the extra jingle of coins in my pocket, always gave the small stash to my parents. My dad never questioned anything but my mother was concerned. I was happy I could make their lives better. I didn't realize the cost to me and my soul. The smells of decay were in my nose twenty years later. They would never leave. Not even if I spent the rest of my life as Baron Witherspoon.

By the time I relieved Dave, Hickey was lying in his bunk fast asleep. It seems the wicked and the evil sleep easier.

"Has he said anything?" I asked.

"Nah. Not to me or George or Ray. At one point he looked at me and kind of smiled. He was nodding his head, like he was disapproving of the way I was dressed or something. Then he just lay down and curled up and went to sleep. Sure does snore loud."

I was trying to figure it out in my head how much time to keep him here before we brought him up to the county jail. Chief Taylor had been on the phone with the district attorney to tell him what kind of case we had. It seems we were going to need a little more evidence because he wasn't as certain of a conviction as we were. It was up to me to put together a report that would be solid enough to allow us to transport this jackal. The thought that stuck in my head that scared me the most was having to let him go. That would bring everything down on me like a tornado ripping through a barn. I wasn't about to let that happen.

Chapter Thirty-Three

Hallett sat behind Childers' desk drinking twelve-year old Scotch in a crystal glass. It was a relaxing moment, almost celebratory. He had successfully diffused a police investigation into the death of a known felon. He had been instrumental in the arrest of a gangster who was undermining a lucrative operation in theft, gambling, booze, and prostitution in a five state region. He had personally put order back into a chaotic world. Or perhaps it was the other way around.

Martin Childers sat opposite his desk. The smirk on Hallett's face was because he knew this mouse of a man was thankful he still had a job and was allowed to continue running Kanotex. Hallett placed all the blame for Hickey getting out of control square on Childers, although he never said it aloud. It was his lax approach to the various Chicago thugs that turned a simple scenario into a possible gang war. Even though Hickey clamed loyalty from only half a dozen men, it was enough to start shooting up the town and becoming the kind of scene the northern cities were used to. Arkansas City had its share of the criminal element but on a quiet and more peaceful basis, a controlled environment of graft. No one knew and no one cared. They liked it that way.

"You gonna get involved?" Childers sipped from his glass, happy to be off the hook.

"No need to. Any cop will recognize what they've got before them and send that little Mick bastard away for good."

"What about Witherspoon?"

"What about him?"

"I think he might be trouble."

"You're forgetting about Chief Taylor."

Martin stood up, leaned backward to stretch, placed his glass on the table, and started to appear less like a child and more like a warrior.

"That old man is getting tired of his job. He couldn't care less. You thought he'd shut the damned thing down. The way I see it he's letting Witherspoon run the whole outfit. And that boy has got it out for me."

Hallett stood up, placed his glass down, placed his hands firmly on the desk, and leaned forward. "You worried about Witherspoon, Martin? Or maybe you're worried about me?"

"This isn't over. Don't think for a moment it is. Even if Hickey gets sent away, Witherspoon will be looking at us like a hawk watches a squirrel. And if he comes after me, I'll gladly give him you."

Hallett's smile outdid the Cheshire Cat. Politicians had that ability. He knew when to be generous and when to be firm. Childers was brought into the fold because he was a business man in search of easy money. The councilman knew guys like this preferred no difficulties and very little involvement. Unfortunately, there was both right now. It was up to Hallett to ensure this one little mosquito didn't annoy the real big wigs.

"It'll never get that far. I've got enough people and

enough options to keep this thing under wraps. Hickey goes away. Witherspoon runs into a dead end. That's all you have to worry about."

"But what about…"

"That's all you have to worry about."

It was a brick wall with Hallett. He could tell the pathetic businessman was worried, at first about the potential police investigation that could send him to prison and wasn't buying any of the tough talk. Politicians needed to maintain a strong and respectable front to make you feel one way so that you would ignore what they were actually doing. What was truly necessary was to prevent the riffraff from knowing and seeing who was behind them. The grandfather on the hill. The real money and the real power. That was a threat they would never see coming and could never fight.

****

Brennan waited a couple of days, checking out the flower shop and the hardware store. The cops had allowed the owner of the flower store to reopen and had never even gone into the hardware store. He felt the tunnels were safe.

He got word out to Pat McArdle and Jimmy O'Donnell to meet that night. It was late October, with Halloween and Arkalalah just around the corner. It was getting cold, not as cold as Pretty Boy Floyd who had gotten gunned down in a cornfield in Ohio. Brennan knew they had wheat and alfalfa fields in Kansas and that would have been just as bad.

Jimmy had his collar turned up and kept blowing into his cupped hands. A couple of swigs from a bottle in one of the cases might have helped. Pat was fuming, eyes almost glassy, huffing heavily, like a wasp that had gotten nicked by a crotchety old lady with a broom.

"They ain't gonna keep him here," Sean started. "They're gonna have to move him up to Winfield."

"So?" Pat was not looking for drama or good story telling. He just wanted to get to the point.

"Only one road up far as I know."

"No, there isn't." There was a bit of a high pitch squeal the way Jimmy blurted it out so fast. "There's a guy between here and there that's got ammo Jake buys from. Some old timer with a farm. I been once with Jake. He took this back road that kicked up dirt and pebbles a lot but he said no copper knew it."

"If anybody knows it, Witherspoon does." Sean first had to figure how the cops were going to bring Jake up before constructing a plan to help him escape. After all the jobs they'd pulled and all the money they had on account of Jake, he wasn't about to let him get caught up in a Kansas jail for the rest of his life.

"Suppose we do grab him. Where do we go from there? We can't come back here. We'll have to leave all this loot behind." Sean knew Pat wasn't being contrary; he just wanted a plan and a direction. The comfort of working out of a small town as a base was apparently gone for good. They all figured they would have to start over again. Maybe someone was getting a notion to just leave and go somewhere to have a normal life, whatever that meant. Perhaps find a woman and settle down. There was talk some guys had done it only there were no names or any notion whatever became of them. Maybe they were just stories other gangsters told when they got tired and worn down and knew their lives were coming to an end.

"We get to Joplin. I've been in contact with a lady there says she can put us up for as long as we need. Then, I figure Springfield is a good base. We do this right, it's a clean break."

Pat blew out his indignation in a big puff of air. Not a single decent city was mentioned. Why didn't Brennan say New Orleans or, hell, even Oklahoma City?

"More rubes and hicks. You're talking deeper into the woods, Sean. You're talking lakes and forests. I don't fly that way. I need some pavement under my feet. I ain't much for fishing and hiking and whatnot. Might as well tell me to go straight." Pat had been down in Kansas longer than any of them. He figured a year out of the Windy City and everything would blow over. Maybe get the word to go to New York and start fresh there. But the word never came. Just like Jake. He was feeling forgotten and lost.

"It's just until…" Sean was genuinely trying to smooth it out.

"Just until what? That's what they told me in Chicago. *Just until things blow over, Pat. You'll do fine. We'll bring you back when we're ready.* Well, guess what? I'm still here."

They stood there in silence. Sean knew he couldn't run the operation by himself, knew he needed Jake. Pat was feeling frustrated and desperate. Jimmy was just along for the ride. Without all three of them working together, Jake was going to rot away in some jail. There would be no fake guns carved out of wood and colored with black shoe polish. No jailer was ever going to fall for that again. They had to figure out whether getting Jake out was more important than simply going their own separate ways.

****

Jake had never been in a position like this before. He had been picked up and questioned by coppers in Chicago over one beef or another, held in a trick room for several hours under hot lights, fined for a minor infraction. Just about every time, George would send a mouthpiece if it was a heavy rap or just let Jake ride it out and he'd be out by dinner. This time he was cornered like a field mouse in a barn by yapping dogs that wanted fresh meat.

Eric Kimble, the kid from the neighborhood who couldn't cut it as a gangster, had the cushy job pretending to be a beloved local boy who was now a respected police officer. This wasn't about law and justice but plain out revenge. Jake couldn't really get upset about that because it was the way he himself lived. Jake could remind Eric about the time shortly before the war when their mutual friend, Johnny Arbuckle, was killed by a hack driving too fast. It was a terrible accident in Eric's mind. To Jake, it was an unforgiveable sin. Eric went with Jake and they followed the guy home. He witnessed Jake empty his gun into him after making the poor slob beg for his life. The papers said the man's wife, holding their infant child, saw everything from the front door. At that point, the war was a welcome relief for Eric.

Jake realized there were only two options: either the guys were going to make some kind of plan to get him sprung, in which case he would have to keep his eyes and ears open; or he was going to jail based on very little evidence and largely the prejudice of a bunch of farmers on a jury. He had to be prepared for both.

Whatever happened, he would not give these backwoods coppers any satisfaction, any information, anything to hang their weary hats on. A deadly smile would be more than enough to create a little mystery. He knew as well that no one would believe the truth about Officer Witherspoon. He was their beloved war hero who had just saved the city from a violent gangster who was now trying to besmirch his reputation. After thinking about it further, Jake had to admire Kimble's whole set-up. He had accomplished everything he had intended. He left Chicago, left the gangs, found himself a job with a regular life. The only thing he had to sacrifice was his face. And his identity.

Chapter Thirty-Four

It took a while to set all our ducks in a row. First, Big Ray drove up to Winfield to compare the fingerprints on the knife, the fingerprints we got from "Mr. Hale" and the Record of Arrest and Prosecution sheet of Jake Hickey sent by Wirephoto from the Feds in Chicago to the District Attorney in Cowley County. We got a match confirming all three were the same. Based upon the time of death as determined by Dr. Brenz, we calculated the best scenario of the crime given the fact that Hickey would not provide a solid alibi we could check. It seemed a little flimsy but it was possible to draw inferences and possibilities. There was very little information about Heather Devore directly, and she was not identified by the Chicago police when contacted over the phone by Chief Taylor. Local merchants were able to verify she had expensive tastes based on her many purchases. Given all of this circumstantial evidence, they sent Big Ray back to Ark City with instructions to transport the prisoner.

While I had concerns regarding Chief Taylor, I realized I had nothing concrete to justify them. Outside of a couple of phone calls, he had stepped out of the way of the investigation and didn't try to hinder it. He practically told me to do what I needed to put this rabid dog away and insinuated I didn't have to stop there. Whatever it was, I felt a little bit more relaxed with him, enough to bring him in on our plans for moving Hickey.

"We'll use two cars on this. I'll drive Hickey. George, you and Dave follow closely behind."

"Maybe we should drive up ahead of you," Dave suggested. "You know, spot an ambush that way."

George McAllister, who had been on the force almost as long as me, shook his head, holding his chin in his hand, and looking at a local map we had spread on the table.

"What is it?" I asked.

"Let's not underestimate who we're dealing with here. Remember reading those reports last year about that massacre up in Kansas City? These guys just started blasting away and the only thing that happened was the guy they were trying to help got killed in all the gunfire."

"Jelly Nash. Yeah, I remember reading about that. You got an idea?"

He used the fingers of both hands to point out separate routes on the map. "This is the traditional road to drive up to Winfield. They know about that. But over here is the farm road that Ray's always talking about. Probably took it up and back when you went."

Ray nodded. It wasn't an authorized route so he didn't want to admit too much. "What if we use one of the cars as a decoy?"

"So, I drive Hickey in the main car through the countryside and the other car goes up the main road."

"Those guys know you," Dave chimed in. "You're recognizable, if you know what I mean." He was either referring to my presence or my face. In either case, I knew what he meant and didn't take any offense.

"He's right," George continued. "Look, Baron, Dave kind of looks like Hickey."

"What are you saying?" Dave seemed unnecessarily offended.

"You're short and you got dark hair. If you wear similar clothes and keep you're hat down, they're not going to know it's you. I'll drive Hickey up after you guys leave."

I liked where George was going with this idea but I wanted to make it even more secure. "Let's try this. We'll have a car waiting out the back of the station house. Hickey will be handcuffed and gagged so he can't scream out. Ray will help me out with Dave dressed up as Hickey tomorrow morning. We'll make a big to-do about it. Bring him out the front door. But George, you and Hickey will have already left before sunrise. It's a longer way up there by that farm road so we should arrive at the courthouse around the same time."

"What about me?" Ray asked.

"You don't look like anybody," George said, a silly smirk on his face. "You get to stay behind."

I was confident about our plan. What I couldn't settle into was just leaving Hickey up in Winfield. They didn't know him like I knew him. Short of shooting Hickey in the middle of the street, I knew we had to follow the law and turn him over for trial. From what Chief Taylor told me, the District Attorney was prepared and felt confident. I had to let that rest.

The day had become so busy and had slipped away from me. I had forgotten how hungry I was and decided to grab a big dinner. I stopped by Daisy Mae's and saw Larry Hammer hugging his favorite seat at the counter.

"What do you know, Larry?"

"Hey, Baron."

Larry was the chief engineer at the Shell Refinery. I swear there wasn't anything he couldn't fix or manufacture given the necessary tools. He could even make the tool if he didn't have it. He was one of the few locals that had nothing to do with any of the bad element in town, at least not directly. Rubbing elbows with someone is not quite the same thing. Whereas he might not go out of his way to pass on any gossip he might have heard, he kept his nose clean. That's really all you could expect from anyone.

When Dixie finally sashayed over to me, I smiled. It was the first time I had done so in weeks. She was full of sass and could talk straight up with any rough and tumble bird that walked in and get prim and proper with the church ladies. You don't run the best diner in town as a frail flower.

"What'll you have, good lookin'?"

"How about the Blue Plate Special, Dix?"

"Meatloaf."

"Wasn't that the Blue Plate Special last week?"

"Didn't you like it?"

I nodded. Larry was laughing at me, knowing that I could never win with Dixie.

After I had stuffed myself to the gills, I headed home. I was going to need a good night's sleep for the long day ahead. I was walking with my head hanging down, eyes practically halfway closed. Just as I turned the corner onto my street, an older woman approached me, walking quickly with a kind of mild desperation. She was wearing a heavy wool ankle length skirt and a woven shawl pulled tightly around her shoulders. She had a lace scarf on her head. It was a dull faded white and seemed slightly worn. She had etched lines in her face, around her eyes and mouth, and blood-red eyes, not the kind where you're too tired but rather full of intense anger. She looked as though she were weighed down with the heaviness of life and fought back at every step of the way.

"You are Officer Witherspoon?" Her accent was heavily European, perhaps German, a trace of which I caught from Abram Dutcher. In her case, it sounded like someone who had just come over to this country.

"Ma'am?"

"I'm Karla Frankl. The professor wanted me to remind you to use extreme caution." It seemed strange that Dutcher should be sending this relic of a woman as a messenger.

"Is there something particular he wants me to be aware of?"

"The chances exist that your friend will not see the inside of a jail and that he will do everything possible to avoid such a circumstance."

"I'm aware of that."

"He is currently the biggest threat to the safety of the people in this community. Focus your attention solely on him. Everything else is secondary."

"I know, but..."

She didn't wait for me to continue and walked by without waiting for a response, harshly hitting my arm as she passed. The dispatch was delivered and her job was done. I wasn't sure what kind of a warning Dutcher had meant to pass along. Perhaps it got lost in the translation somehow. I had to try to feel confident about the arrangements we made. I had no other plan, no other idea I felt comfortable putting into place. With all the talk of corruption and payoffs on the force, I couldn't take a chance by bringing anyone else in on this. It was too late to change anything. We had to continue on the course we had set and hope for the best.

Chapter Thirty-Five

Dave Morton wore a suit similar to Hickey's that he borrowed from one of the snazzier dressers on the force. I had the handcuffs on him and he had his hat pulled down low. Chief Taylor and two other officers escorted me and my *prisoner* out the front door to my car. It was about ten in the morning and we expected to get to the Cowley County Courthouse in a little over an hour. George McAllister and Jake Hickey had already left more than two hours prior. Given the farm roads they were taking, we figured they would get there just slightly ahead of us.

The policeman in Winfield weren't made aware of our ruse and actually started roughing up Dave before I had a chance to put them wise. Once inside, I unlocked the cuffs and identified my fellow officer. The sergeant in charge, a bruiser named Starkey, tried to pretend as though he was annoyed but his sly smirk gave him away. The mood changed sharply when he announced the real prisoner had not yet arrived.

"Those roads are pretty treacherous. Lots of rocks and divots. Could take them longer than you expected. Hope they don't bust an axle." He made sense but I was still concerned. George was a good driver and very focused on this assignment. It was approaching noon, and I knew there was no possible way it would take four hours to get here.

The district attorney wasn't anywhere around. Their chief of police was in meetings every time I asked about him. I was missing an officer and not getting any assistance in the matter. Dave and I took matters into our own hands and set off down south, hoping to cross tracks with George.

As we approached, I remembered the spot from a prior time escorting a prisoner up to Winfield. There was an encounter with a rugged looking farmer who seemed to not want anyone looking into his business. George's car was sitting there off to the side of the road. George was in the front seat, a bullet hole in the middle of his forehead. Hickey was nowhere around.

"Ambush?" Dave could barely speak the word. It sounded like he was choking on barbed wire. The car wasn't in the middle of the road where it would have been if he had been caught off guard. It didn't appear from the dirt in the road the car had stopped suddenly nor had it been shot at. It was as though it had pulled over in a designated location and only the driver had been surprised by the turn of events. If my assumptions were correct, it was an ambush of sorts, just not the kind I felt good about considering.

I turned back suddenly and went to the car. Dave followed but grabbed my arm. I swiveled around with a look that must have made Dave worry about my sanity. I was doubting it myself. "Where you going?"

"We're going back to Ark City. Hickey's loose and he's too much of a wildcat to cut his losses and run. He's coming back."

"For what?"

"For me."

I drove because I wanted to do something with my

hands. I wanted to feel like I was in control. I wanted to pretend it was Hickey's neck in my hands and I was strangling the life out of him. At that moment, I didn't think of Baron Witherspoon or being a police officer or doing what the law said I should do. If needed, I was going to do what was right, regardless of the consequences.

It took a while for the rage in my head to subside, the way a tornado passes over a field and leaves destruction in its path. I had to focus enough to consider what he might do. Given we were a small town, I could only imagine Hickey had been able to lure desperate men who were looking for enough of a bankroll to leave not only Arkansas City but Kansas as well. If the reports of bank jobs and robberies in our area were the work of his men, they could easily see Oklahoma City, Dallas, and even Joplin had more for excitement than our small bump on the map. These men, his gang, would be the ones to try to convince Hickey to leave, indicating it wasn't worth going back, regardless of what they had to leave behind.

That wouldn't be the case. Hickey and I went way back. We had a history. For whatever reasons, he could blame his circumstances on me even though it was Bugs Moran who had dropped him like a hot potato and never came to his rescue. Chances are that had Hickey stayed in Chicago, he would have wound up dead a lot sooner. Maybe that was better to him than dying a slow death in the middle of nowhere.

The funny thing was I had felt that same way. After the war, after recovering from the experimental surgery on my face, I knew I had nowhere else to go than Kansas and nothing else I could be other than Baron

Witherspoon, whose father was grateful to have him home to work the farm. If that had happened, I saw myself running to the police and the judge and declaring who I was, telling them to ship me back home and get rid of the liar in their midst. It was only when I realized I couldn't go back that I tried to make a life for myself. Hickey could never do that. He wouldn't have even tried.

"Someone's got something on Chief Taylor. We can't count on him to help but he won't stand in our way."

"What are you saying, Baron?"

"Childers and Hallett are the money and the influence in town but they don't run things. Someone else does. Someone with a heck of a lot more power and influence than we realize. I just haven't figured out who that is. The point is they don't want Hickey around."

"What are we supposed to do?"

There were so many random thoughts floating through my head I had to just say it all in one fell swoop. "Only two places I can think of Hickey going. One is Phil Garmes."

"Garmes? The kid's nothing. Why would Hickey go there?"

"Garmes will stick him in a room in The Gladstone, especially if there's a gun in his face. He might go to Junior's but Hallett will have some of his boys watching there. I don't think he is crazy enough to think this is the Old West and Dodge City and all that malarkey and have a shootout in the street. What we need to do is draw him out."

"How?"

I hadn't figured that out exactly. All I knew was I would be the target.

Chapter Thirty-Six

It was especially cool out, more than fall and giving a preview of winter. Jake was wearing a worn jacket and pants that were frayed at the cuffs. It was designed to hide his appearance from any potential gang members. In a way, it was Witherspoon's attempt to humiliate him. Jake was the flashy dresser, the sharp suit in the crowd. Jake was the one with good taste. To be dressed as a panhandler was an insult. He was willing to let himself be made a fool knowing full well it wasn't going to last long.

Baron was up early, at the station, making sure Hickey changed into these clothes, giving George last minute instructions. They had gone over it so many times it seemed pointless to say anything again.

"You're taking Summit as far out of town as it goes, then connecting with Farm Road 15, jog west to Farm Road 177, then north onto Farm Road 96 all the way into Winfield."

"I've got it, Baron."

"It's just that it's a long stretch..."

"I've got it." Baron nodded, realizing he was sounding like a mother hen.

Hickey said nothing. He didn't have to. There was no reason to intimidate Witherspoon/Kimble. Not now. That time would come. He looked down, looked away, looked anywhere but at the man who had put him in this position. He may not have been the only one. He was one of many. They would all pay. Jake would see to that.

They didn't feed Hickey any breakfast. George had two cups of strong coffee and a blueberry muffin Baron brought him from Daisy Mae's. Once they got up to Winfield and dropped Hickey off at the courthouse, Baron planned on taking George and Dave for lunch. He figured he would do something for Big Ray later.

It was a little after 7:30 in the morning that George McAllister drove out of the back of the police station and headed north. He had the window cracked, letting in some of the morning air. It almost felt like the dew was sneaking in through the open window. There was a lot to keep in mind: the plan Baron drew up and also the plan Sean Brennan had advised him about. It was worth five thousand dollars to get punched in the face and the stomach a couple of times. Brennan had made it clear Hickey was leaving town, heading to Kansas City, at least for starters, before moving further north, back home, back to where he was comfortable.

It was simple. George pulls over at a point just a few miles south of Winfield where a farmer friendly to their cause is waiting with a new vehicle and a change of clothes. Brennan, McArdle, and O'Donnell would be there. It wasn't specified as to whom would knock George around but it would appear as though someone got the jump on him. And they did.

George pulled the car to the side of the road at the designated spot right where the old grizzled farmer had waved him off. Suddenly, the farmer was pointing a gun in George's face. He didn't expect it all to go like this but he went along.

"Give him the key." The farmer's voice had the quality of broken glass. George did even more than he was told, unlocking the cuffs from Hickey. "What now, Jake?" George asked, politely.

Hickey reached into George's jacket, pulled out his gun, and backed out. With the farmer still pointing the gun at George, Jake came around the front where Sean Brennan had suddenly appeared. At this point, George expected to be dragged from the car by Hickey himself and given the once over.

"You got the flivver?" Hickey asked Brennan.

"Yeah. It's just as he said it was," Brennan commented, indicating the farmer.

Hickey came around to the driver's side.

"What now?" George repeated, this time with a slight crack in his voice. A single shot rang out, hitting George in the forehead. He slumped down in the car, never expecting Hickey's play. Brennan rushed up to him. The farmer turned the gun on Brennan.

"Jake, what are you doing? We had a deal with the guy."

"The guy was a cop. A friend of Kimble."

"Who's Kimble?"

This was a private war, one Jake Hickey felt no need to clarify to his gang. They would follow his instructions with no discussion or argument. "We're going back," Jake declared. Sean grabbed his arm as Jake started back to the new car.

"Back? Why?"

The farmer turned the gun on Sean. Jake looked back at him and shook his head, indicating he should back down from Brennan. "This thing's not over, Sean. That cop is not going to stop following us. Ever. We're going to put him down like a sick dog. Then we go for Childers."

"Jake, these people are protected."

Jake turned suddenly, moved toward Brennan, cocked his gun, then placed the barrel on Brennan's forehead, just about the same place that poor George McAllister was shot.

"Nobody's protected from me. Do you understand? Do you?" Brennan shook his head. There was no need to say anything to Jake and certainly no reason. This was a runaway train he had jumped on months ago and there was no getting off now.

Jake lowered the gun and moved in closer to Brennan. The farmer was just a thug who was pleased by a fifty dollar bill and would do anything to show his appreciation. Jake knew Brennan was the kind of gunsel he needed, the kind of man who hated cops as much as he hated working in a refinery or a packing plant. He was the type of guy who was fed a line about cooling off until the heat was over and was left hung out to dry. A good worker, a loyal guy, who deserved better than a small town in Kansas. Just like McArdle and O'Donnell. Just like Hickey.

"He doesn't know about this. We've got the jump on him. We head back and settle in, we can get him when he comes back to town. None of the other cops are worth a damn without him."

"What makes him so special?"

Jake had reasons both personal and practical. Both were too extensive to explain here. It came down to putting away the one man who would continue to come after him no matter what. Either that or die trying. There was no more Bugs Moran, no more Chicago, no more North Side Gang. He had outlived everything he knew. That didn't necessarily make it worthwhile. He was almost forty. Deanie, Hymie, the Schemer—none of them made it as far. He couldn't tell if he was blessed or cursed. None of that mattered. All he knew for sure was that Eric Kimble was going to be looking for him once he came across this scene. If he needed to go it alone, he would. These other guys had nothing to do with this.

"He's my problem, not yours."

Brennan had never been the loyal type but he recognized what Hickey had done for him and the others. Literally trapped in a small town with no connections and little funds, Hickey's planning gave them all a substantial bankroll. Whether they wanted to continue robbing or leave the heat for good, Sean knew that sticking around for an Old West type shootout wasn't going to be good for anybody. At this point, Hickey preferred it this way.

The farmer drove them back to the barn where McArdle and O'Donnell were waiting. Brennan got in the car and drove off with the guys, never saying anything further to Jake, never explaining to the guys. There was an Olds sitting in the barn. It ran but felt like it was on the verge of coming apart. It seemed like an appropriate vehicle to make an entrance. Or an exit.

Chapter Thirty-Seven

It was time to think like a rat.

I had lived in Ark City for nearly sixteen years. I knew the streets. I knew the people. All the ways of the past, the ways of the big city, were long behind me now. It was a shame because that was what I needed now.

Hickey had few options. I figured he would stay low and try to watch me, try to follow my moves. With that in mind, there was now a dull buzz in the back of my neck feeling like a hot needle. His watchful eyes.

Ray didn't take the news of George's death well. I didn't tell him my suspicions that he had sold us out because it would have hurt and confused him even more. Tears welled up in his eyes but he never let them run. He had some doubts whether he could handle this job when it got rough. I knew that. But there was a change over him, a big sniffle, a clearing of the throat, and then his shoulders getting cocked back like a pistol, and a "Let's go" to punctuate his resolve. He was going to show me he knew how to be a good cop.

We marched down to The Gladstone. Ray stood out front like a knight in front of a castle. Dave roamed the lobby while I located Phil Garmes standing behind the front desk. I grabbed by his shirt and forcefully escorted him to the back room.

"Where's Hickey?" I said harshly, only two inches

from his face.

"What?"

"Where's Hickey?"

"I...I..." He kept shaking his head.

A fine layer of sweat appeared on his forehead, almost like a sheen of morning dew but only hot and sticky.

"Hickey. Where is he?" Phil looked like he was starting to melt. He was either useful to me or a waste of my time. I decided to find out. I drew my gun and stuck it against his forehead. "Where's Hickey?"

"He...he...came by early this afternoon."

"For what?"

"He told me to give you a message."

"What was it?"

"He said it's not over."

Jake was playing games with me. Phil couldn't help any more than that. I figured he would be leaving town once this thing blew over. He wasn't going to be happy living here regardless of which one of us came out on top.

The next thing we did was go to Hallett's office in town. Before he was a city councilman, Hallett spent his time as a lawyer. You couldn't tell one type of graft from the other. He still maintained an office in the center of town, his showy presence making it seem like he was a Roman emperor. Guys like that fail to remember their history lessons, especially the ones about a bloke named Julius Caesar.

Ray and Dave took their positions much as they did at the hotel. I walked right past his secretary's desk while she tried to verbally hold me back. Unfortunately, she didn't have strong enough words or a voice to do so. A man in his forties with a pencil thin moustache and wearing a gray suit was sitting opposite Hallett who noticed the blank look on my face.

"Why don't we pick this up later?" Hallett said to the client with a warm professional smile. The gentleman rose, reached across the desk to shake Hallett's hand, then turned and walked past me without making eye contact. Hallett then generously motioned toward the empty seat. I opted to stand.

"The professor told me I shouldn't worry about you. Said Hickey was the one who could cause the most trouble."

Hallett smiled as though he didn't have a care in the world. Dr. Brenz could have just told him he had a month to live and he probably would have had the same smile, pasted on his face while his oily tongue formed lies covered in rose petals. I wondered if being a lawyer and a politician gave him that smile or if he was born with it.

"Ah, so Dutcher is still around."

"You knew he was."

"I suspected. But he had lost his power long ago. The good people of Arkansas City were not going to accept a Hun running gambling and whoring in their town while a war was going on. It would have been…unpatriotic."

"I don't have time for this, Hallett. I need to find Hickey."

He leaned forward, crossing his hands in front of him, and lowering his voice even though there was no one around who would listen or care.

"Without even planning it, I have stumbled across the perfect scenario. I have two thorns in my side, neither of which really cares about me at this moment. You see, Hickey was not like the typical gangster who came down here to take advantage of our generosity and hospitality. He was a stubborn pig-headed Mick with a bad attitude. And because of him, he drew out your suspicions about me far more than your own inclinations. Naturally, I am far more upset with him. Nevertheless, however this plays out, I will be happy. If you are able to eliminate Hickey, that nuisance will be gone and you will forever run into a brick wall trying to investigate me. You simply have no viable resources. If, on the other hand, Jake kills you, he will be treated like a rabid dog and will be gunned down like Dillinger. Either way, I will be quite content."

He leaned back in his chair, keeping his hands crossed in front of his belly, while that big smile spread across his face. "For what it's worth," he said, "I'm pulling for you."

The wickedness he exuded got my stomach tangled up and about made me want to vomit. I had no time for moral repulsion. For that matter, the concepts of Law and Order were not foremost in my mind either. The only thing right now was to find Hickey and kill him. If it were necessary to take the rap afterwards, I would do it.

The three of us stood outside Hallett's office. Ray and Dave looked at me as the wheels spun in my head. I looked up and down Summit Ave. trying to come up with a notion. "The guy we killed in the flower shop, we ever identify him?"

"No. He didn't have any identification on him. No one stepped forward and none of the businesses in town claimed him." As usual, Dave was able to report the facts and keep things clear.

"What was he doing there?"

"We figured he was robbing the place." Ray's eyes were squinting like it was noon on a summer day. At first, it almost appeared as though he had a headache. Then he spoke his mind with assurance.

"No. That was no robbery. I know Mr. Clark. He runs the shop mostly because he loves flowers. Says he wants to make the world more beautiful. He doesn't have enough cash in the till for the likes of those guys."

Dave had a look on his face like he was trying to get an idea to pop from the back of his head to his mouth.

"What is it?" I asked.

"You've heard the stories."

"What stories?"

"Tunnels. Connecting some of the shops. What if these gangsters found them and were using them?"

"For what?" I wasn't challenging Dave so much as getting him to work his idea out where we could all hear it.

"Who knows? Storage. Gambling. Escape."

All of those made a lot of sense. If the reports of the major robberies in the area were the work of a small gang working out of Ark City, an underground storage area would come in handy. And if the heat got too great, it would be the perfect place to hide.

"Ok, so let's visit Mr. Clark and see what he can tell us."

It was Ray clearing his throat that made us stop for a moment. "Is it just going to be us?"

I was proud of him for overcoming his fears but I needed him now more than ever. There were so few people I could trust at this time. "Unfortunately, Ray, every cop we work with is not on the up-and-up. There are things going on in this city that make it look like Little Chicago."

"I know that," he replied, demurely.

"Okay, well, here's the way I see it. This is a tough situation. We could get shot or killed. Now, that's a fact. If we can't be sure whom we can trust, it's more than likely we're going to run into it bad. It may not look so good just us three but I'll take my chances with you two more than anyone else I know." I smiled, like a big brother. He smiled back. I was scared but confident. It felt just like the war.

Chapter Thirty-Eight

The thought of rumbling into town, making a big noise, commanding attention and respect titillated Jake Hickey. This was how it was in Chicago. Even if you wound up with a touring car filled full of triggermen with tommy-guns chasing you down, you knew you were something. The New York guys, Coll and Diamond and the Dutchman, all drew enough attention based largely on the fear of others. That would have been an ideal entrance. Knowing you were feared was the pinnacle of success.

Unfortunately, Ark City was not as big as Chicago, did not have an elaborate network of streets and locations where like-minded characters could gather and feel safe. He recognized a few guys from the Windy City but he couldn't tell whose side anyone was on. The most important thing was getting to Kimble and taking him out. Once he did that, the real big timers who ran this joint would see he was not a man to be trifled with for anything. They would realize he had the brains and guts to carry out any job that would fatten their wallets. He would finally get the respect he felt he deserved all along.

He dumped the rig on the south side of town near what appeared to be an abandoned house. Several windows were broken and none of the doors were locked. He stepped in slowly, looking around for anything that might be useful. There were no personal effects, no clothing or kitchen utensils. There was a heavy oak dining room table with no chairs and a sideboard empty of any china. Upstairs, a bed stripped of all the linen and a small end table with a drawer sat awkwardly in the center of the room. He thought about lying down and getting some shuteye until he opened the drawer and found a Bible. Considering it bad luck, he left the house altogether.

He needed to get a hold of the Garmes kid, the only person in town who he could coerce into getting him what he needed. It was useless going directly to The Gladstone considering that would be the first place Kimble would go. He remembered Garmes stepping out back to smoke and figured it would be easier to keep an eye out in an alley. Looking at his watch, he figured he still had some time before Kimble and the other policemen figured out what had happened. That stupid cop actually thought he was going to give him cash or, dumber still, take him along. He considered himself lucky knowing no big city cop would have fallen for that. He knew he couldn't count on all of them being so stupid.

It was late morning and Jake was starting to get impatient. He was thinking how he could get to Kimble, how he could either ambush him or force him to face off against him. This was a different place, one that didn't allow for much maneuverability. Too many public places. Too many opportunities for bystanders to get killed. He needed to figure out a plan to take Kimble down. He should have thought of it before he had come back. But he didn't and now he was here and here is where it would happen.

Phil looked like he didn't have a care in the world. Probably because Jake was finally gone, Hickey thought to himself. The kid was going to be surprised. Jake's pace quickened as he tried to catch Garmes off-guard. He had his gun in his pocket, grabbed Phil's arms, and jabbed his ribs. "Did you miss me, kid?"

"Mr. Hale." Phil's voice cracked like he was going through puberty.

"The case I left you to hold for me. You still have it, right?"

A small brown leather satchel with straps had emergency funds and additional guns and bullets in case the heat rolled in. He hoped Garmes had been too scared to turn it over to the police, even after what happened to Heather. He knew he couldn't count on the stash of guns in the tunnel, especially if the cops finally figured out that whole arrangement. This satchel was just enough to get him out of a jam.

"Yes, Mr. Hale."

"Where is it?"

"It's behind a stack of crates in the kitchen pantry."

"Let's get it." Jake pushed the gun further into Phil's ribs while twisting his arm and pushing him inside the building. He looked back behind him and all around. He knew he had time but also was aware how quickly it could disappear.

Phil led Jake into the pantry through the kitchen. In the back corner of a storage room there were wooden crates stacked up alongside potato and onion bins. The area smelled like a cheap Irish soup kitchen and made Jake angry remembering how poor he was as a kid, even after his father was able to get steady work from the local gangs and mobs. Nothing was better for them in spite of what his father claimed. The old man might not have had to work in the meat packing plants but he was raking in more dough and putting elegant meals on the table, as far as he knew what elegant meant. His dad was gone half the time, leaving his mother to keep them alive through whatever paltry allowance his father would leave her. The damp, musty smell sent him into a bitter spiral.

The dust on the satchel proved it hadn't been moved for a while. Jake lifted it up and placed it on the top of the potato bin. He quickly undid the strap and wrenched it open. Five thousand in cash and two guns, both Browning .32 automatics, with boxes of bullets, stared back at him with a smile. Right now, bullets were more important than money.

Jake whipped around to face Garmes. "I've seen Kimble with a younger girl. Who is she?"

"Kimble? Who's Kimble?"

Jake was getting flustered. He felt everyone should understand him implicitly. "Witherspoon. Officer Witherspoon. Tell me: who's the girl?" he spat tersely and impatiently.

"You mean Beth Handy?"

"Who is she?"

"Her father owns the millinery shop."

"He goes with her?"

"I suppose so. I-I don't know."

It didn't matter if she was Baron's sweetheart or anything else. She was someone he cared about, and Jake figured Kimble didn't care about too many people. They were more alike than either one of them would care to admit even if it was true. They were focused, directed, had a sense of what was right and wrong, at least to each other, trusted few people, and counted on fewer. They had each taken a long and desperate road to get to this very point, a place they hadn't known about nor heard of before. This is where it was going to happen, their showdown, their final stand.

"He'll be coming back here," Hickey said, a slight upturned smile on his face reminiscent of *Crazy* Jake. "When he does, you give him a message for me. You tell him it's not over."

Jake cocked his gun and held it squarely in Phil's face, which was now covered in sweat. He started to close his eyes not wanting to see the bullet he thought would end his life. Jake made a loud grunt that forced Phil to become alert and keep his eyes open.

"Bang!" Jake's smile looked larger than a circus clown.

Phil was frozen. Jake ran through the way he had come in and left through the alley. He had to get to the milliner's shop before the rest of the policeman got back from Winfield.

Chapter Thirty-Nine

It was hard to think of a flower shop as a place for criminals. Then I was reminded of Dion O'Banion, that crazed bootlegger who thought chrysanthemums were as beautiful as a well-planned murder. Most of these guys had expensive clothing and jewelry and cars but no real sense of style or class. Whatever money could buy that they never had seemed like the best thing to have. Then again, I didn't really have much room to talk when it came to confused sensibilities.

I was fairly certain Mr. Clark was not involved but I didn't want to press him too hard and scare him off. If he had been threatened by Hickey or his men, he needed to know for sure we were on his side and would protect him. I was hoping he would believe me.

We knew time was of the essence. Hickey was just crazy enough to come back to town and challenge me, thinking that somehow, something from the past warranted revenge, even though I did what I could to keep away from him. Maybe it was getting out, leaving, trying to do something noble, something he didn't have the stomach for and could never do, which got under his collar. I doubted he had any virtues like that despite thinking he did. It's funny how the way we look at ourselves is often not the same as the way others see us.

The three of us entered together, with Ray and Dave casually looking around to see if anything was amiss.

"Mr. Clark, have you got anyone new working for you?"

"Why yes, Baron. How did you know?"

"Local guy?"

"No. 'Fraid not. One of those poor souls who'd lost everything up north. Said he was getting tired of working in the refinery and just wanted to be around something beautiful for a change."

"Is he here now?"

"Hasn't been in for two days. Beginning to worry about him."

"Mr. Clark, you ever hear of those stories about the tunnels?" Dave interjected. He sounded like a young son asking his father to tell him an old timeworn tale.

"Only stories."

"You mind if we look around, Mr. Clark?" I asked gently. "I think those tunnels just might be real and maybe right here."

"Amazing! You go right ahead, Baron." He went back to dusting the counters and sweeping up, trying to present a clean and respectable environment.

We weren't sure what to look for but I felt there was something here. This was not going to be like a door to the basement in your house. Whoever had built these tunnels was intent upon secrecy and privacy. Something that seemed out of place, something that wasn't part of a typical storage room was going to be our key.

At the far wall was a workbench where Mr. Clark trimmed flowers and created arrangements. A woven rug, nothing more than a heavy tarp, was in front of it and extended fifteen feet or so in front of the table. I could understand the idea of catching debris but it seemed as though this piece of fabric was covering more than it needed to. I motioned to Dave and Ray. We got on the opposite side and lifted it up. The door in the floor revealed stairs going down, into the tunnels that had been, up until that moment, nothing more than stories.

I looked around the storage room and found a small lantern, enough to give me three feet of light in front of me. It might not have helped in the case of an ambush but I was guessing it wouldn't happen down there.

"I'm going first. Ray, you follow. Dave, stay up here and keep a lookout for Hickey."

"What makes you think he's not down there?" Dave sounded a little like he was losing his confidence.

"I don't know. It's not a place he'll be able to get out of quickly." I turned to Big Ray knowing the tunnel would challenge his height. "Keep low but stay at least ten feet behind me. Move slowly and listen for anything. You okay?"

"I'm ready, Baron."

The most important thing was to listen. Without sufficient light, we had to hear any movement and couldn't wind up making more noise ourselves. After I had gotten about ten feet away from the stairs, I stopped and waited for Ray to get to the bottom. The lantern was providing even less light than I figured.

The walls were damp and cold. My hand found a door, the wood filled with splinters. I tested the knob and found it locked. I came across two more doors, which were also locked. Whereas Hickey could have been in any one of them and come out to shoot me in the back of the head, I was confident he wasn't going to sacrifice his own life, given the fact that Ray was right there.

My shoes scraped across the dirt floor as I inched forward. I kept convincing myself Hickey was not here, that he wasn't waiting to gun me down, that all of my life was not pointing to this one sad and dark moment. Then again, maybe Life was going to pay me back for my impersonation. It wasn't enough I should be so facially scarred that I didn't really know who I was anymore but that I would suffer a violent death surrounded by cold earth not so different from the trenches of so many years ago.

My hand felt an opening and the lantern showed on a large room with several crates. I recognized the labels on some as whiskey and bourbon. A few suitcases stuffed with papers were strewn on the floor. The back of the room led out to a set of railroad type tracks that obviously led to another opening somewhere. If Hickey's gang was responsible for all those robberies, this was more than likely where they stored their stash.

Something colorful caught my eye in the black darkness that I was finally getting used to. I turned the lantern toward the far corner of the room. A red wide brimmed ladies hat with a black silk sash tied in a bow sat on a box high up on a set of crates. I stood on a wooden box to reach for it. When I first took notice, it seemed out of place in here, a musty room with the remnants of gangsters. When I looked inside at the label, I understood why it was there. It was from Handy's Millinery.

I knew his plan.

I threw down the hat, ran back out of the room and toward the stairs. I rushed past Big Ray, almost knocking him over. Using just my memory, I ran straight through the tunnel, forgetting to offer Ray the light to help get back. I climbed to the top of the stairs just as Ray got to the bottom. I told Dave, "He's at Handy's Millinery. He's got Beth."

Chapter Forty

Hurt 'em where it hurts the most. That's the way they got Frankie Yale. Mysterious phone call, said something was wrong with his wife. Any guy's gonna go bonkers and forget himself, and that's exactly what happened. Eric, in Jake's mind, had gone soft over these rubes, especially the sweet little daughter of the hat shop owner. Heather had talked about her often, given the number of times she shopped there. Cute kid who always had something mushy to say about Officer Witherspoon. The kind of thing that made him want to puke. That was exactly where Jake would drive a nail into Kimble's heart.

He was certain everyone would expect an old-fashioned shootout in the middle of the street. But he wasn't as wild as *Two Gun* Alterie and as hot headed as Hymie. Sure, they may have called him *Crazy* Jake but what they often forgot is that he never flew off the handle. Except maybe with Heather. Once or twice. Or more often than that if he really gave it some thought. He knew he was nothing like the way they thought. He was sure of it. Almost sure of it.

Jake had enough time to retrieve his satchel from Garmes at The Gladstone, grab one of Heather's hats from the room—which was closed off due to it being a crime scene—and drop it off in the main room in the tunnel. It was a breadcrumb, a hint, a clue, a tease, something to let Officer Witherspoon how it was going to go down. A hostage, a shield, something he cared about more than himself. Jake would put him to the test and see exactly how much he cared about these people. Find the weakness and aim for it. Hurt 'em where it hurts the most.

****

The town was getting ready for Arkalalah. Pretty soon there would be booths and stalls set up in town, local vendors, clowns and musicians, a whole bunch of men, women, and children roaming around and having fun. Right now there was the quiet before the storm.

A door to Handy's Millinery led out to the alley. I couldn't quite remember how their back room was set up and whether or not Ray or Dave would have a clear shot inside or just wind up making more noise. It might have been better just to have them positioned out back if I was able to force Hickey to run. At that point, I was concerned what either one of them might do if that happened, if they came face to face with Hickey while he was holding Beth tightly in front of him and a gun to her head. I had to believe in these guys. I had to trust them to do the right thing at the right time.

The plan was simple: they were out back and I would approach the shop from the front. I wasn't going to be this noble knight and go in there without a gun, prove I was unarmed and give in to him. That would have marked me as a mutt, a stray dog worthy of nothing and needing to be put out of its misery. Beth would just have to understand my front of bravery. Even if she didn't, everything I needed to say and do was all about getting her and her dad out of the store safely.

"I don't like it," Dave said. "Just you going up there by yourself? He'll shoot you down."

"There's only three of us. I need you both out back. Yeah, I know he wants me but he wants to get out of here as well. Trust me, if it comes down to it, he'll run before anything else." I made myself believe that to assure these two who had stayed by my side. The truth was this was the Battle of the Argonne Forest all over again. Everything was dark and dense; bullets were flying everywhere; there was no problem losing your sense of direction; and it was a fight to the death.

****

It was late morning, shortly before noon. Jake walked casually down Summit Ave., hat pulled down but not so much as he looked like he was trying to hide. The streets were sparse. He looked around slowly and carefully, like an owl watching a squirrel and tracking it's every move. He was certain there would be time before Kimble and the other policemen got back to town after realizing what happened. He was certain he had time to set up his trap.

He entered the millinery quietly, not wanting to come bursting in like the Feds in a distillery. He surveyed the store, saw Beth standing at the counter talking with her father, no one else in the store. He moved toward them before they could even notice.

In one swift move, he hit the old man on the head with his gun and grabbed the girl's arm tightly. She let out a gasp and started to scream before he showed her the barrel of the gun.

"Lock the door."

He guided her to the front door where she pulled a key from her dress pocket and followed his instructions.

"Back door, too."

They moved like they were floating on air to the back room where she followed his instructions. He brought her back toward the entrance of the store. They stood behind the front counter where they could duck down if Kimble or the other cops were foolish enough to just start shooting. Hickey was in a good place. He had the only thing Kimble cared about and would have to fight to get back.

As far as Jake was concerned, Kimble had grown weak. He had given up his neighborhood instincts for survival. He was a pawn and a patsy. Who knows? Maybe it was the war that had done it to him, the facial scarring, or maybe it was this farm life, away from the lights and glimmer of the big city. Either way, the strength Hickey had retained proved to be useful even here. However, even he, too, was starting to feel dulled and slowed by the lifestyle. It was just this one last thing he needed to do before he could get back to the life he really wanted.

"What are you going to do?" The tremor in Beth's voice made it crack and sound less like the lilting sparrow that was typical for her.

"We wait."

"For what?"

Jake smiled and licked his lips. "For the squirrel."

Chapter Forty-One

I was breathing so hard I thought Dave and Ray could hear it. I had to remain in control and think through things clearly.

I knew what we were going to do, but it was best to say it out loud. Instead of an assumed plan, it's a fact, something real, because other people heard it and know what it is. We could have run the risk of talking ourselves out of anything but I knew Beth was in there, probably being held roughly by a man who really didn't care about her life, just what he thought she meant to me. Make no mistake about it: I like Beth a lot, and maybe Baron Witherspoon liked her even more. She looked up to him/me like we were some kind of hero. She might have had a notion of being a hero's wife but, as far as I was concerned, she wasn't the girl for me. I wasn't sure such a woman existed. My goal was to get to Hickey and then get Beth out safely. I was not going to reward either one of us with a marriage proposal if it turned out that way.

"You guys split up. Get to the alley by both the north and south ends. Go as far out of his vision as possible. Let him focus on me. After you're gone from his sight, he'll practically forget you. And whatever you do, don't you both stand at the back door. Bullets can go through wood, right?"

Dave and Ray nodded, then turned to walk off. I

grabbed Ray's arm and turned him toward me for a moment. "I'm counting on you." I said it with an air of confidence because I knew he needed it. We all did.

They stayed close to the shops on our side of the street, trying not to be as noticeable, while I stepped off the curb, in the clear and open, a perfect target. I could barely see each of them when they got to their respective ends of the block. I was sure Hickey couldn't see them from his vantage point. I gave them a few minutes to cross the street and work their way down the alley. Then, I started walking across the street, crouched down, zigzagging my way. I wasn't going to make it easy for him.

****

Hickey held a vise grip on Beth's arm. She kept squirming. It was just a natural reaction. Her head was bobbing like a rag doll, her hair getting into Jake's face, which annoyed him because he was trying to get a good look out the front window to see Kimble.

With his hand that held the gun, he pushed her head to the side, hopefully getting her to realize she was not doing what he expected. In doing so, the hold on her arm tightened.

"Quit shaking your head," he blurted.

"You're hurting me."

"I'm gonna hurt you a lot more if you don't quit shaking your head."

She stopped suddenly and looked him straight in the eyes. The reaction to her pain was putting her in jeopardy. She would have to learn quickly how to deal with it if she wanted to get out of this alive.

Jake watched the two other cops disappear in the background. The mid afternoon sun was causing shadows on the storefronts across the street. The only thing he saw was Kimble step out from the curb, look in opposite directions, and then start moving toward the millinery shop while crouching low.

There was no need to shoot through the window. That would have given away his position, making it just a bit easier for Kimble to put a fix on him. He had the girl and he could wait for Kimble to come to him.

"How do you want it to end, Hickey?" Kimble's voice still sounded like it was at a distance, maybe twenty-five or thirty feet. Jake moved his head to one side, trying to catch a glimpse of him. A car was parked just out front. The most likely place for Kimble to be for cover.

"Oh, I think you know," Hickey shouted back. Without shooting through the window, he had given away his position.

****

The car parked out front was my first goal. I could stay low behind it and be within ten feet of the door. The sun was shining enough it was making it look dark inside. I couldn't quite see where he was. I figured he might be behind the front counter, which was about fifteen feet from the front door. There were large glass windows on either side of the door that also had glass at the top. From the car, I could get to the door and be down behind the wooden part. Then I remembered what I reminded the guys about.

I knew I needed to distract him, keep him focused on me, forget about Dave and Ray. With them back there, the best I could do, when it all started, was to keep shooting and give them time to get in. And not let Beth get shot in the process.

"How do you want it to end, Hickey?"

"Oh, I think you know."

"Me dead and you leaving town?"

"That would be fine by me."

"You might get the first. You won't get the second."

"I don't know. I've got this girl with me. Seems you got a thing for her. Wouldn't want her to wind up in a coffin."

"You shouldn't have come back."

There was a long pause. He didn't have a quick answer. Maybe he realized I was right. Unfortunately, it was too late for anything else.

"But I did," he replied, his voice thick with a salty bitterness.

It was then that the shots rang out.

****

Despite what Dave and Ray had been told, they met up exactly at the back door to the millinery and realizing there were no windows to see into the back room. If Baron had been right, Hickey was probably up front with Beth, taunting and trying to have some kind of showdown. Dave held his ear to the door but whatever sounds he heard were muffled.

"What do we do?" Ray asked.

Dave had the experience and knew about situations like this but he seemed to go blank. Baron liked him and trusted him because he kept his head cool in tight spots. He would have been ashamed to have Baron see him now.

Ray reached for the doorknob and tried to turn it. It was locked. The transom was too high up even for him. He kept looking at Dave for answers but got vacant looks.

"You figure Baron's gonna make his way to the front?" Ray continued.

"Yeah. Pretty sure of it."

"So, who makes the first move—him or us?"

"Who knows? Maybe Hickey will."

Ray looked both ways up and down the alley. He wasn't looking for anything other than an idea. "I think it should be us."

"What?"

"We bust in and that'll be a distraction. It'll give Baron a chance to get to the front of the shop."

Dave was shaking his head. "Beth could get shot."

"Look, Dave, we've got no way of knowing what's going on. We've got to make it happen. It's got to be us."

Dave nodded. He turned toward the door with the shoulder opposite his gun hand. The door gave way after a solid thrust with his body. Dave fell through the door to the right. Ray stepped over him to the left and could see through the interior doorway to the store. Hickey and Beth were crouched behind the counter.

****

Jake knew Kimble was right. He shouldn't have come back. He had put together a good gang, smart, efficient, ruthless, able to knock off banks and jewelry stores. They had cash, enough of it to move on to another city, maybe not as big as Chicago, but something a little more lucrative than Arkansas City, Kansas. He had double-crossed a foolish greedy cop and escaped from a man who was pretending to be someone he wasn't. He was free and clear.

There was just too much betrayal to deal with.

George Moran, *Bugs*, his boss, his confidante, the man who helped him rise in the ranks of the North Side Gang, the man who tried to protect him after the St. Valentine's Day Massacre and after Capone's arrest and indictment, basically sent him away, banished him to a place so unlike him, more than likely to prevent him from taking over. George was getting weak, getting soft, getting scared. This wasn't protection and safety. This was exile.

Heather wanted more than he could get her in this small burg. She couldn't accept the fact he needed time to get them both out of there. She blabbed her way to her own death, a pawn in a game of sinister men.

And Fate had caused him to come face to face, so to speak, with a man from his boyhood, a kid he trusted who only wanted to leave the neighborhood and get as far away as possible. Too many people had pushed Jake Hickey around that he had no recourse but to push back.

He didn't mind the shouting match with Kimble. What he was waiting for was an opportunity to shoot him down like a dog. A loud crash behind him caused him to turn suddenly. Through the doorway to the back room, Jake saw the tall cop, the lanky kid. He shot at him. The kid ducked. The other cop jumped up in the doorway. Jake fired again, hitting him in the shoulder. That's when the shots came from the street.

****

First one shot, then two more. I had heard a crash and a thud somewhere in there. Dave and Ray had come through the shop by the back door. I didn't know who shot first but I was guessing it was Hickey. I had to move now.

I maneuvered from the car to the door, crouching below the glass part. I jumped up and saw Hickey firing behind him. Beth must have still been down behind the counter. I smashed the glass and shot at Hickey.

He turned and fired back. I rose, hugged the side of the door, and spun to fire back. He got off two more shots to my one.

He started to reach down behind the counter. I knew he was trying to grab Beth, use her as a shield. I couldn't let him do that.

I broke through the door and fired off a shot that missed him because he was ducking down.

He stood straight up.

I had my gun pointed at him.

The shot that was fired didn't come from my gun or his.

Big Ray had stepped into the store and got off a clean shot to the back of Hickey's head from about five feet away.

Hickey slumped over the counter, blood flowing over the front like a waterfall.

I looked up at Big Ray, the kid who didn't want to play basketball but rather be a cop. He nodded, his eyes wide, confident he had done the right thing.

Chapter Forty-Two

I went out to Chief Taylor's farm when I heard he had resigned. His wife graciously pointed me toward an old shed in the back of the house. He was wearing overalls with no shirt, heavy leather gloves, sweat pouring down his face as he took apart some kind of contraption with copper tubes and galvanized containers. He turned to me, took of his gloves, shook my hand, and smiled.

"We were in danger of losing the farm on account of not being able to afford anyone to work it. This still was about the only thing bringing in any money. Childers found out about it somehow and, well, I think you can guess the rest."

"Doesn't mean you have to resign?"

He let out a great sigh, one of relief, from a man at peace with the world or at least with his world. "It's time. Getting too rough out there. Besides, Lester Richardson's a good man. Tough and fair. The way you like it."

I hung my head knowing he was right. I wondered whether or not his way was the right way for me.

"You got this Hickey fella. Maybe that'll discourage them Chicago boys from setting foot down here. And I wouldn't get too riled up about people like Childers and Hallett. Their day'll come soon enough."

I had a lot of admiration for the man. He had great

instincts. I was going to miss that.

Ray and I visited Dave at the hospital. He was shot through the bicep and lost some blood. Doctor said he'd have to work that arm quite a bit to get his strength back. He didn't seem to mind too much getting all the attention from the nurses.

As we were leaving the hospital, I felt I needed to say something to Ray, tell him I was proud of him, like an older brother. Then it started to seem awkward and I simply patted him on the shoulder as I headed down to Daisy Mae's.

Dr. Brenz found me in a booth having a club sandwich and a cup of coffee. He sat opposite me, smiling in a way I hadn't seen him do in years. "You've come a long way, Baron." There was a funny way he said my name, as though he was emphasizing it, trying to make it stick. "I'm convinced all your wounds have healed. All of them." I looked him straight in the eye. He was squinting and nodding lightly, trying to speak to me without words. "I know what you might be thinking, that it's time to move on. But this town really needs you. They need Baron Witherspoon." He reached out, placing his hands on top of mine, continuing that slight nodding. As far as he was concerned, the past was better left where it was.

After he left, I sat there for a long time when I was done eating. Sixteen years had passed. I understood who everyone was, even myself. It seems that it's not as important how you start but where you wind up. I could never have guessed a city boy with big dreams could wind up being happy in a small town doing right by others and thinking less of himself. I had always been concerned I could never tell who I was by looking in the mirror, that the scars had obliterated Eric Kimble but the face didn't look like Baron Witherspoon. Then I realized those were just names. It didn't matter what you called me as long as you knew who I really was.

I certainly was no farmer. I didn't have much of a notion of taking a wife and raising kids. By the same token, I couldn't see myself wearing silk shirts and fancy hats, walking down city streets with bright lights. All I figured on doing, as long as I could, was keeping the peace in this town and trying to give other people a chance to live a good life. Maybe that's all I was supposed to do.

When I went up to the front counter to pay, Dixie waved me off. "No need. While you were sitting there daydreaming, a funny little man walks in and pays for you. Said not to bother you about it."

"Did he give his name?"

"Nope."

"I wonder why he did that."

"That's the kind of stuff heroes get."

"Aw, come on. You're pulling my leg."

She reached over the counter and pinched my cheek. "The hell I am."

I walked around for quite a bit, despite the cold chill of the evening. The only thing I could hear was the click of my shoes on the pavement. It was quiet, not in the sinister way when things are going on that you don't know about. It was more the sound of tranquil nights and sweet dreams.

The silhouette stood just in front of my rooming house. I knew it was the funny little man Dixie mentioned. It was Abram Dutcher. "Thanks for paying for my dinner."

"A small token of my appreciation."

"For what?"

"It's been a long time since I've encountered a man of honor. That alone is worthy of respect."

"If you say so."

"I do."

He didn't move and I wasn't sure what to say. I figured I would try my luck and see if I could impose upon his generosity a little further.

"You think you might be able to, let's say, point me in the right direction with regard to Hallett?"

"From what I hear, the syndicate is keenly interested in towns like this. They have no patience for small-minded men like the councilman or Mr. Childers. But don't worry. They won't get in your way. They'll leave you to take care of the drunks and vandals."

"What about you?"

"I'm a remnant from a lost time. I have no more place here."

"Sometimes I feel that way, too. But I was just told otherwise." Dr. Brenz weighed heavily on my mind. Whatever he knew or thought he knew didn't matter. He encouraged me to look forward.

"Are you familiar with the Irish playwright George Bernard Shaw?"

"No, sir."

"He said 'We are not made wise by the recollection of our past but by the responsibility of our future.' It is your time now, Officer Witherspoon."

He tipped his hat and walked off into the darkness.

My road was ahead, toward the light.

A word from the author...

I studied film-making and creative writing at the University of Miami in the '80s, was involved in the Boston Poetry Scene in the '90s, and am a former president of the Kansas Writers' Association. With an emphasis on crime fiction, I have stretched out into experimental fiction, always looking to push the bounds of the craft.

I live in a 100+-year-old Victorian home in Wichita, Kansas with my wife, Shelia, and two cats, Mongo and Rupert.

http://tikiman1962.wordpress.com

Thank you for purchasing
this publication of The Wild Rose Press, Inc.

If you enjoyed the story, we would appreciate your
letting others know by leaving a review.

For other wonderful stories,
please visit our on-line bookstore at
www.thewildrosepress.com.

For questions or more information
contact us at
info@thewildrosepress.com.

The Wild Rose Press, Inc.
www.thewildrosepress.com

Stay current with The Wild Rose Press, Inc.

Like us on Facebook

https://www.facebook.com/TheWildRosePress

And Follow us on Twitter
https://twitter.com/WildRosePress

Made in the USA
Lexington, KY
11 January 2017